繁華 散盡.........

When the splendor is gone

廖玉蕙 散文　中英對照

欣賞中文與英文雙美

　　中譯英本非易事，除了了解字面意義外，還要懂得作者筆下的意境。中華民國筆會多年來秉持「團結優秀作家，提高創作水準，譯介本國當代作品，促進國際文化交流」之宗旨，在歷任主編殷張蘭熙、齊邦媛、宋美王華、彭鏡禧、張惠娟、高天恩、梁欣榮等教授主事下，精選優秀的中文作品，翻成英文，推廣至全球各地愛好中文之美的人士。多年來，政府致力推廣優質國內文學作品，希冀藉由台灣優秀的文化競爭力，以期與國際接軌，因此九歌出版社與譽滿全球的中華民國筆會合作，精選好看好讀的名家文章，並配合精確的英文翻譯，讓國人同時領略中英雙種語言之美，與政府拓展國人國際觀的理念目標，相輔相成。

　　本系列以名家作品為主，首先推出多位知名散文家的散文，計有張曉風、廖玉蕙、席慕蓉等。本書為名散文家廖玉蕙的作品中英對照《繁華散盡：廖玉蕙散文中英對照》。廖玉蕙老師以其女兒之親親、以教師之仁愛，以作家之尖銳的筆觸，展現其生活散文特色。

　　內容上，精選廖玉蕙老師名作。收入她以疼惜的心情，寫下兒女最傷痛的記憶、最苦悶的升學經驗的〈如果記憶像風〉。〈一座安靜的城市〉是三進金門的感觸。在〈繁華散盡〉及〈遠方〉中談論對父母親的懷念。幽默細數親子之間互動關係的〈你不知道我成績有多爛〉、〈我為卿狂〉、〈情深似海〉，以及對於年紀的體悟〈年過五十〉等共9篇散文。而編排上則採用中文與英文對照編排方式，讓愛好中文散文者，閱讀名家作品，豐富自己的用字遣詞，增進寫作能力。學習中文人士可藉由精采的散文作品中英對照，了解道地優雅的中文；閱讀英文及翻譯研究者，忠實領略到文學之美。期待這一套書為中西方文學打開交流與了解之門。

——編者

目 錄

一座安靜的城市

City of Silence

柏松年／譯

Translated by Jonathan Barnard

汽車在木麻黃、油加利及各色各樣不知名的行道樹環伺的柏油路上行駛，除了偶爾幾聲的牛叫及鳥鳴外，整個城市似乎沉浸在沉沉的睡夢中。號稱戰地的金門，因為過度的安靜，給人一種錯覺，彷彿在靜默中潛藏著不為人知的殺機。不管是古意盎然的珠山、充滿南洋風情的得月樓、古宅縱橫的蔡厝，甚或望遠鏡鳥瞰下的民俗村，一逕是端凝莊重、簡潔素樸的風貌。

二十餘年前，我念研究所時，

和一群年輕的夥伴，同時應邀參觀金門。

原以為逐波踏浪，將會是一趟旖旎浪漫的旅程，哪知洶湧的海浪，使得上岸的臉孔，個個變得慘無人色。十年前，我再度造訪金門，和二十餘位作家同行，甫下飛機，迎面便是端正的舉手禮和親切的「老師好！」幾天中，我的那些被分派到金門服役的學生的殷殷接待，使得我的聲望，陡然在作家群中水漲船高。然而，首次金門行，醉翁之意不在酒，當然也不在山水，情竇初開的男女，除了盈盈的眼波外，哪容得下堅固無情的壕溝？再次的金門行，熱切的和學生敘舊言歡，根本亦未曾把戰地的固若金湯擺進眼瞳。問起金門印象，恍恍惚惚，一派模糊，只剩了炎陽烈日和參天古木。

When I was in graduate school more than two decades ago, a group of young friends and I were invited to visit Kinmen.

Expecting a romantic journey and enchanting environs, we had visions of loping through gentle surf. Instead, we met surging seas on the way over and staggered ashore with green faces. Ten years ago, I returned to Kinmen with a couple dozen of writers. Upon leaving our plane, I was greeted with a formal military salute and a chorus of warm voices: "Hello, Teacher!" For a few days, former students of mine posted in Kinmen for their military service treated us as their coddled wards—and consequently gave a sudden boost to my reputation among my fellow writers. On that first trip to the island, as young men and women just discovering romance, we were less interested in Kinmen than we were in each other. With all of our amorous gazing, where was there time to survey battle trenches? On my next visit, my former students and I whiled away our hour happily reminiscing, so that once again the real Kinmen never came into view. When asked later for my impressions of this battle-tested fortress at sea, I could offer only vague descriptions about a harsh sun and towering old trees.

今年九月，三進金門。因為國家公園解說員的精
心策畫，並仔細隨行解說，金門因之展示了不同的面
貌。無論歷史古蹟、傳統聚落、宗祠家廟或者蝶鳥林
木，都顯得生趣盎然、饒富情味，使得三出金門時的
我，覺得意猶未盡、行囊豐盛。

所有的行程，都遠離人口密集的都會。大部分的
時候，我們看不到任何人跡。那日，到歐厝參觀是
唯一的例外。聽說一場戶外寫生比賽正進行著，從旅
邸出發時，大夥兒戲言是去參加畫畫比賽。古意十足
的巷道中，已有若干家長領著孩子，擺好架式。空氣
裡，充滿著節慶般的歡愉。孩子們露出一本正經的表
情，邊看著景物，邊動手勾勒著，當觀眾湊上前去，
一窺究竟時，多半的孩子會假裝若無其事，然而，臉
上霎時泛起的紅潮，則偷偷透露了心裡的忐忑。幾位
沉不住氣的家長，按捺不住宰制的本能，始則以委婉

In September, I went to Kinmen yet again. This time, thanks to the carefully planned itinerary and detailed commentary of National Parks Administration guides, Kinmen presented a new face to me. Everything we saw—from the historical relics, traditional residences and clan shrines, to the forests filled with butterflies and birds—proved fascinating; even for a third-time visitor such as myself, it was a short though fruitful trip.

The itinerary kept us far from the highly populated areas of the towns, and most of the time we hardly came across anyone else at all. The sole exception was the day we visited the Ou family traditional compound. We had heard that an outdoor drawing competition was being held there, and as we left the hotel we joked about competing ourselves. Along the antique streets and alleys, where the air was filled with a festival like joy, parents were leading their children to set up and get ready. With diligent concentration, the children began to look back and forth between their subjects and their own renderings of them. When bystanders closed in for better looks, most of the young artists feigned indifference, only to be betrayed by blushing cheeks. Finally, the parents' efforts to contain their own domineering natures flagged, and they started,

的建議指點，繼則以負面的言詞批評，從取景、構圖
到顏料的使用，都絮絮叨叨；嚴重的，索性捲起袖
子，取過色筆，開始為畫面潤色起來。被搶去畫筆的
孩子，有的嘟著嘴和多事的母親理論著；有的乾脆和
弟弟打鬧遊玩起來，留給望子成龍的母親盡情發揮的
空間。

　　幾位隨行的畫家，也混跡於人群中，獵取中意的
景致。他們把作畫的孩子及家長畫入作品中，也讓自
己成為孩子們作品裡的風景。因為流連景物而延緩上
車的他們，被同行者揶揄是因為參加頒獎典禮之故，
毒舌派的作家當然沒放過這個難得的機會，鄭重其事
宣布：

　　「雷驤先生得第三名，蔡全茂先生得佳作。」

ever so gently at first, to make suggestions. Soon the trickle turned into a stream of nagging negativism that covered everything from the choice of subject matter to the techniques employed for outlining and coloring. In the more extreme cases, parents simply rolled up their sleeves and picked up the pens themselves. Left empty-handed, some children pouted and argued with their meddlesome moms. Others seemed happy enough to join younger brothers in raucous play, leaving the hopeful mothers ample space to express their own visions.

There were some painters in our group, and they scattered amid the crowd looking for things to catch their fancy. Drawing the children and parents into their works, they in turn entered the drawings of their subjects. Caught up in what was going on, they were late getting back on the bus, and some of their fellow travelers began to joke that they had been participating in the awards ceremony. A writer of the forked-tongue school took the opportunity to solemnly announce: "Mr. Lei Hsiang was awarded a bronze medal and Mr. Tsai Chuan-mao an honorable mention."

頓一頓，清清喉嚨，惡作劇地加註：

「第一名計十三位，第二名共十八位，第三名則有五十位，參加者一律列名佳作。」

接著，汽車在木麻黃、油加利及各色各樣不知名的行道樹環伺的柏油路上行駛，除了偶爾幾聲的牛叫及鳥鳴外，整個城市似乎沉浸在沉沉的睡夢中。號稱戰地的金門，因為過度的安靜，給人一種錯覺，彷彿在靜默中潛藏著不為人知的殺機。不管是古意盎然的珠山、充滿南洋風情的得月樓、古宅縱橫的蔡厝，甚或望遠鏡鳥瞰下的民俗村，一逕是端凝莊重、簡潔素樸的風貌。

車子在珠山錯落的古厝間停下。迎著我們的，除了形同中古世紀廢墟的房子外，就是正中的一塘池水。夏日已近尾聲，卻仍時刻聽聞蟲聲唧唧，我們像

Then, after a throat-clearing pause, this footnote: "There were 13 golds, 18 silvers, and 50 bronzes. All participants were guaranteed at least honorable mention."

Finally our bus left on its journey along asphalt roads lined with whistling pines, eucalyptuses and other trees whose species were unknown to me. Apart from the occasional water buffalo's moo or bird's chirp, the whole place appeared to be fast asleep. Kinmen seems almost too silent, and in conjunction with its war-torn history this tends to engender a false sense of some looming potential for violence. Everything we would see in Kinmen was simple and dignified—from historic Chushan and the Moonlight Pagoda, with its strong south sea flavor, to the orderly rows of buildings at the Tsai family compound and even the bird's-eye-view via binoculars we had of the Kinmen Cultural Village.

Our bus stopped in front of some old residential compounds in Chushan. The residences, which appeared to be virtually medieval relics, were grouped around a pond where the insects were still going full blast despite summer's imminent departure. We felt like

一群冒失的入侵者，無意間闖進了一座猶自沉沉入睡的城市。

　　天色是淺淡的灰，塘水裡映照的也是幾抹淺淡的雲影，幾乎看不到天光。一群人，下得車來，如辭根的九秋蓬般，在環繞的瓦舍危牆間自在行走。畫家們選定了角度，便在紙上揮灑開來；一位認真的民俗研究者，拿著簿子和筆，以過人的求知慾，孜孜叩問，即便地上亂長的野草都不輕易放過。我信步遊走，穿越一幢幢雖然老舊卻仍煥發精彩古色澤的老屋，除了少數幾幢屋子因院落間曝曬的衣著，讓我們知曉應該仍有人居住其間外，幾乎讓人錯覺根本是個廢棄的村莊！正納悶著當地的人都到哪兒去了？忽然一輛古舊的腳踏車從遠處馳過，騎車的童子，頻頻回首在後頭徒步追趕的另一童子，因著距離，沒能聽到什麼對話，卻從嬉鬧的姿勢裡，彷彿聽到恣肆的笑聲！整個村莊，因之陡然有了生氣！

a group of reckless invaders who had unknowingly marched into a sleeping city.

The sky was a light gray, and the clouds' vague shapes reflected on the pond's surface. So diffuse was the light that its skyward origin was barely discernable. A group of us left our bus like thistledown breaking free in autumn, and wound our way past the tile-roofed buildings and courtyard walls. The painters found pleasing angles and began to put their visions of them on paper. A diligent folklorist, armed with pen and notebook, displayed a curiosity so extraordinary that even the wild grasses found it hard to escape his inquiries. I wandered among the gracefully aged houses, which were superb examples of traditional architecture. The whole village seemed quite deserted, with only clothes-drying racks in a few of the residences' courtyards providing any evidence to the contrary. Just then, an old bicycle zipped by in the distance. The child rider turned his head to look back at another youngster, running behind. We were too far to take in their conversation, but we could almost hear carefree laughter in their merry motions. Immediately the village seemed full of life!

　　窄巷的盡頭,赫然是一幢年久失修的樓房!隔著高高的圍牆,可以想像牆內盤根錯節的老樹根及青苔遍布的階梯上都被厚厚的落葉覆蓋著,閣樓上的窗口邊兒,彷彿還斜倚著一位綺年玉貌的少女,正將癡情的眼光凝睇著遙遠的地方……正無止盡的騁馳著想像,冷不防,一陣涼風飄然而至,我不禁打了個寒顫,急忙快步離開。

　　池塘的另一邊兒,樹倒屋傾,蛛網糾結。我們排除糾纏的枝枒,小心翼翼地踩過地上的青苔,來到過氣的將軍府。殘破剝落的大廳,樑柱歪斜,叱吒風雲的過往,徒然剩下幾個鐫刻於壁間的姓名,無端讓人想起廉頗老矣,尚能飯否?再是蓋世的彪炳功業,終歸還是要隨著四季的流轉,被逐漸淡忘。將軍府的鄰居,隱隱傳來壓抑的電視聲,我探過頭去,從木製窗口看到一位老太婆正佝僂著背,面對電視機打著瞌睡,太平時序裡的韶光,似乎正以平靜遲緩的步伐悄

At the end of a narrow alley, we came upon a ramshackle old house that must have been abandoned many years before. Outside its tall garden wall, I imagined what it was like within—the leaves scattered thickly across the gnarled, intertwined roots of the old trees and on the moss-covered steps, and upstairs a beautiful lovesick girl, leaning against the frame of an open window and gazing into the distance… A cold gust jarred me from this stream of fantasy, and I hurried off.

On the other side of the pond, cobwebs covered the tumble-down buildings and fallen trees. After smashing our way through a thicket, we carefully tread across a stretch of moss to reach an abandoned general's residence. In the dilapidated main hall, where the paint was peeling and the pillars and beams bent out of shape, all that remained of its commanding past was a few names carved on the wall. It brought to mind the Warring States-era general Lian Po: "Now that he's old, how well does he digest?" No matter how grand and glorious one's achievements, all are forgotten in the relentless turning of the seasons. From next door came faint sounds of a television. Craning my neck for a view, I could see an old

然隨著老人勻稱的鼻息，越過蝶飛蟲鳴的庭院，在山水之間悠悠蕩蕩。

地上牛糞處處，偶爾會發現正踩在乾枯的鼠屍上，折翼的小鳥曝屍在怒長的草叢間；葛藤植物不客氣的自窗櫺間穿堂入室；在廣漠的大地上，老天以無言之教，呈現生死榮枯的自然律則，只是，行走於其間的旅者，有否從中得到啟示，則不得而知。

迥異於傳統聚落的得月樓和附近的洋樓群也是金門極為珍貴的文化資產，它的建造印證了中國「錦衣不夜行」的光耀門楣傳統。因為，據說有些洋樓的建構，只為光宗耀祖，並不真正居住。多數的創建者和他們的後代，仍僑居南洋，洋樓常委託親戚代管。當我們在棋盤式井然有序的巷弄間穿梭參觀，見到建

woman, her back slumped forward, who had fallen asleep watching the tube. In this peaceful age, the pace of life has slowed to the even breathing of an old woman who sleeps as butterflies flutter and crickets chirp in her courtyard.

Water buffalo pats were everywhere, and from time to time we found ourselves stepping on a mouse's dried-out carcass. A small, broken-winged dead bird protruded from a lush clump of grass. Vines rudely climbed inside through windows. Across the vast land, God reveals through wordless teaching a law of nature: What is born will die and what flourishes will wilt. But do travelers walking amid these signs gain enlightenment from them? That we do not know.

Though quite unlike Chushan's traditional Chinese residences, the Moonlight Pagoda and western-style structures in its vicinity comprise another of Kinmen's precious cultural assets. Their construction offers testimony to the traditional Chinese idea that refusing to return home to show off a family's newly acquired wealth would be as pointless as "deciding to wear elaborately brocaded clothing only at night in the dark." Many of these foreign-style buildings were, in fact, built purely for the glory of a family's

築的宏偉、建材的講究及格局的新穎時，嘖嘖稱奇聲此起彼落，而一想到那麼精緻的建築竟然無人居住、任其荒廢，又不免喟嘆不已！步行至一處無人居住的大宅院時，不知誰發現院落裡的一株結實纍纍的龍眼樹，高興地呼朋引伴。於是，有人找來採摘長竿，挽起袖子，玩起幼年時偷摘芭樂的遊戲；身手俐落者，乾脆一個箭步，躍上圍牆、爬到樹梢，來個大小通吃。樹下的人仰脖加油，樹頭的人，越戰越勇，一群中年人，彷彿又回到少年時代，歡喜地在樹下分食甜滋滋的戰果。

下午，轉往蔡厝。身為蔡家媳婦的我，一入蔡家廳堂，見進士、文魁、武舉的匾額高懸，竟有著與有

ancestors and have never been used as actual residences.Most of the original builders and their offspring lived in Southeast Asia, and they got relatives to look after these foreign-style houses for them. As we walked through the orderly grid of streets, turning from one building to the next and observing the magnificence of the architecture, the exquisite taste of materials and the innovative layouts, we found ourselves murmuring in admiration. The murmurs turned to sighs of lament with the thought that many of the structures were unoccupied or even left for ruin. Then someone, I forget who, discovered an old longan tree laden with fruit in the yard of a house and called the rest of us over. A few of us got hold of a long pole, rolled up our shirtsleeves, and replayed a childhood game of stealing guavas. Others, who were nimbler, climbed onto the courtyard wall and from there jumped into the branches of the tree. Those of us down below craned our necks shouting encouragement, as those up in the tree got bolder and bolder plucking the fruit. It was like we had returned from middle age to be kids once again, and under the tree we joyously gorged on the fruits of our victory.

In the afternoon we turned to the Tsai Family Compound. My husband is also surnamed Tsai, so when I entered the main hall and

榮焉的驕傲喜悅。外子收拾起一路嘻笑的愉悅神情，端凝肅穆的在蔡厝的十一世宗祠前拍照留影，並弓身入內，對祖先牌位一一頂禮膜拜。正好一位長者背著手，逡巡其間。當我們熱情的告訴他，我們是來自臺灣的蔡氏宗親時，他並無預期的熱烈回應，僅微微一笑，讓我們不免略略有些失望。不過，繼之一想，金門自開放觀光以來，參觀者眾，前來認親的人，何止百千！怎能期待如何驚喜的回應！如此一想，也就稍稍釋然了。

依舊是千迴百轉的街道，依舊是默默不語的院落，只有幾個老人聚在一塊兒，有一搭、沒一搭的輕聲說著話。轉到一個四合院的曬穀場中，赫然撞見兩位年輕人正和一桶子釣來的活魚奮戰著。看到我們，驕傲地向我們展示成果，血淋淋的刀起刀落，為這安

saw, hanging high, carved wooden lists of Tsais who had succeeded on the imperial "Wuju" military exam or "Jinshi" and "Wenkui" civil service exams, I felt a kind of pride and joy. My husband, meanwhile, put away his traveler's grin to be solemnly photographed in front of the family shrine to the 11th generation of Tsais. Then he bowed as he entered the shrine and prayed to each of his ancestors' tablets. Just then, a family elder strolled in with his hands behind his back. When we excitedly told him that we were relatives, Tsais from Taiwan, he merely smiled, evincing none of the enthusiasm we had anticipated. We couldn't help but feel disappointed. Yet on second thought, clansmen from Taiwan must have been arriving by the hundreds and thousands since the government allowed visits. How overjoyed could we expect him to be? Thought about in this light, his lack of ardor seemed quite understandable.

We wound our way as before through the streets and past quiet courtyards. The only sign of life was a group of old folk huddled together, whose conversation sputtered off and on in muffled tones. Then we came upon a courtyard of a traditional Chinese house, and there, where grains would have traditionally been laid out to dry in front of the main hall and between the two forward-

靜的城市妝點了些不同的聲勢，這是作客金門三天中，難得看到的景致，在這看似安靜的城市中，顯得突兀。說起來有些詭異，金門原為前哨重地，歷經烽火洗禮，原本應充滿火砲煙硝才對，怎麼看到拿刀的年輕人，反倒覺得格格不入？是國家公園內的古厝宗祠淡化了火藥味？抑或年輕人口的大量外移，使得除了軍隊之外的人口年齡層急速老化，竟致歲月的腳步亦因之猶疑舒緩起來？

適合旅遊的天氣，些微的風，淡淡的雲，空氣中散發著慵懶的氣息。車子在樹林中奔馳，千奇百怪的樹木從眼簾匆匆掠過，布袋蓮盤據的大池，靜靜仰臥在叢林間。經過了一天半的奔波，在回程的車上，大夥兒都顯得有些疲累，有人在徐徐晚風的吹拂下睏著了。

protruding wings, we saw two young people struggling with a bucket of live fish they had caught. When they saw us, they turned to show us their take and then started brutally hacking away at the fish with knives. The scene, seemingly in jarring juxtaposition to Kinmen's quiet streets, completely altered the day's mood. Yet in retrospect, only our reaction seems odd. After all, Kinmen was originally famous as a look-out post on the front lines of war, a place where battles raged and weapons' smoke filled the air. Why should youths with knives seem out of place there? Had the old buildings and clan temples inside the national park dissipated the smell of gunpowder? Or had an exodus of Kinmen's youth and the subsequent rapid aging of the island's non-military population, slowed the pace of life to a hesitant crawl?

The weather was well suited for touring, with a soft breeze and light clouds, and languor floated on the air. As the bus cruised through the forest, we watched hundreds and thousands of strange trees pass before our eyes. We saw a pond in the jungle that brimmed with water hyacinths. After a day and a half on the bus, my companions seemed a little fatigued, and on the way back from the sights some of them dozed off under the caress of a soft breeze.

天色逐漸黯淡，車子由白天開進夜晚，也開進了和白日迥異光景的熱鬧繁華中。張燈結綵的飯店裡，金門高粱挾帶著豐盛的美食，召喚著每個飢餓的肚腹。然而，想起前日午餐時的深水炸彈威力，不禁隱隱警戒起來。前日，甫下機，國家公園的處長及副處長、課長、祕書、解說員等就一字排開，企圖以深水炸彈的強大酒力威嚇我們這群看似軟弱的文人！頗有左良玉長刀遮客引柳敬亭就席的態勢。誰知，文人、畫家不讓敬亭專美，即刻豪爽地舉杯迎戰，絲毫也不怯場。一頓飯下來，雙方暫時打成平手。原以為一場深水炸彈的拚鬥，勢所難免地要在次日繼續分出高下。豈知，公園處昨日的陣勢原是虛張聲勢，背水一戰的結果，已有多位面臨陣亡的危機。因此，那晚，一上飯桌，不戰自潰，始則顧左右而言他，繼則頻頻討饒！然則，酒量雖有待琢磨，但是，席上殷勤依舊，談起當地山水屋宇、古蹟名勝、一派憐惜，語調中的溫柔，尤其令人印象深刻。

The sky darkened, and the bus rode from day into night, before emptying us into a dazzling bustle quite unlike the day-time's. In the festively bedecked hotel, Kinmen Gaoliang alcohol and a gourmet meal of many courses awaited us. They beckoned to our growling stomachs. Memories of "Deep-water Bombs" we had endured at lunch two days before, however, put on us on our guard. Barely after we had left our plane, a group from Kinmen National Park, including its director, assistant director, various department heads, secretaries and guides, had lined up to drink deep-water bombs with us—to terrorize a bunch of wimpy bookworms! It brought to mind the Ming general Tsuo Liangyu forcing the storyteller Liu Chingting to drink at knifepoint. Little could the park staff have expected us writers and artists to rise to the occasion and raise our glasses without a hint of fear of hesitation! At the end of the meal the two sides had fought to a draw, and we thought that the battle would by necessity be extended to the following day. But it turned out that the park staff had been bluffing all along. Never expecting us to pick up their gauntlet, they found their ranks ravaged by the first day's ferocious fighting. The next evening their lines were broken before the battle had even started, and whenever we mentioned drinking they did their best to change the

　　清代文人張潮曾在《幽夢影》中說：

　　「若無詩酒，則山水為具文；若無佳麗，則花月皆虛設。」

　　將「佳麗」二字改為「朋友」，則庶幾曲盡當日心境！山水、詩酒、花月、朋友，金門之行，樣樣齊全。如此人生，幾回能夠！

　　──原載一九九八年十一月十六日《中國時報》

　　收入九歌版《讓我說個故事給你們聽》（1998年）

subject, trying always to weasel their way out. What they lacked in ability to hold liquor, however, they made up for with unflagging graciousness. They spoke about the island's landscape, architecture, famous relics and tourist attractions with affection. Their gentle voices, especially, left a deep impression on us.

In *Quiet Dream Shadows*, the Qing dynasty essayist Zhang Chao wrote:

"What would be the point of natural splendor if it couldn't be celebrated in poetry and drunken reverie! How meaningless the moon and flowers would seem if there are no beauties around!"

If you replace "beauties" with "friends," then these lines would do well describing our feelings then. Scenic beauty, poetry, wine, flowers, moonlight, friends...our trip to Kinmen had some of each. How many such times will one have over the course of a life?

***"The Chinese PEN"* Summer, 1999**

繁華散盡

When the Splendor Is Gone

盧競琪／譯

Ttranslated by Crystal Allen

這些天，我一直翻閱著昔時的照片，在一本本的相簿中，父親一逕地以他招牌的笑容光燦地面對鏡頭。從年輕到年老，從紅顏到白髮，從山巔到海隅，從打球到下棋，從加州的水綠沙暄，到北海道的冰雪滿地，從人子到人父，甚至人祖……他總是那般興高采烈地擁抱生活。

星月交輝，煙花競麗。

　　母親和我，推著坐在輪椅上的父親，在笑啼喧闐的人潮中，親密地談笑。父親不時地稚氣地仰起頭，指著高處閃爍的燈花，興奮地東問西問。鑼鼓盈耳的街道上，扶老攜幼的，盡是怡然歡愜的天倫圖。涼薄的夜風也趕來助興，和雲集的小攤販上縷縷竄升的炭煙相互追逐嬉戲。

　　許是為這滿路的巧笑新聲所牽引吧！父親突然忘形地自輪椅中立起身來，一不留神，竟仆倒在微雨過後猶自溼滑的泥地上，在迅速蟻聚的人群中，不知是我，還是母親，抑或其他的什麼人，驀地淒厲地狂喊了起來：

　　「流血了呀！流血了⋯⋯」

　　暗紅的血，很快地在父親仆倒的地上，殷殷地蔓

The stars are twinkling in a moon-lit sky. Fireworks are showing off their beauty one after another.

My mother and I are pushing my father in a wheelchair through a boisterous crowd. We intimately talk and joke with each other. My father raises his head in a childlike way from time to time, pointing at some glowing lanterns and excitedly asking casual questions. With sounds of gongs and drums in their ears, people take their parents and children out to the street. Everywhere is a happy family picture. Cool breezes of the night join the cheerful crowd, playing with smoke from many street vendors' stoves.

Perhaps drawn by the sound and joy, my father has been beside himself and suddenly he rises from his wheelchair. Carelessly, he falls down on the muddy road which is wet and slippery after a drizzle. People quickly gather around him like ants around food. Somebody, who could be me, my mother, or anybody in the crowd, suddenly utters a wild cry, "Bleeding! He is bleeding!"

Dark red blood floods the ground around my father. My

延了開來。母親彎下身，輕輕地扳過父親的臉，父親睜開眼，綻開笑靨，朝我說：

「實在有夠鬧熱！」

然後，徐徐閉上了雙眼。我驚懼地大叫：

「爸！」

冷汗涔涔下，我自驚怖的夢中醒來，黑暗裡，眼淚潸潸掉了一臉。不遠處的鄉間廟會，似是印證著我的夢境般，急管繁絃毫不稍歇地歡慶著元宵夜。

那夜，我身處預官考選命題的闈場內。節慶的歡愉在晚餐過後的猜謎遊戲裡達到最高潮。為了稍稍紓解久困闈場、不得返家團聚的遺憾，大夥兒特意布置了餐廳，搬來了卡拉OK。我隨著眾人歡唱談笑，刻意忘卻生命中那樁永遠無法踐履的約定。酒酣耳熱後，麥克風傳到了一位笑聲最響、飲酒最豪的上校軍

mother bows down, lightly moving my father's face toward her. My father opens his eyes, smiles, and says to me, "It is really bustling!"

Then he slowly closes his eyes. Frightened and fearful, I scream, "Dad!"

With cold sweat all over my body, I woke up from the nightmare. My tears kept coming down my face in the dark. There was a gathering in front of a temple nearby. It seemed to echo my nightmare, celebrating the Lantern Festival with the fast and incessant playing of Chinese wind and string instruments.

I was sequestered from the outside world that night, to maintain the secrecy of the exam questions I was preparing for selecting military reserve officers. In the sequestered building there was a dinner party. A riddle-solving game after dinner was the most fun. Then there was karaokee in the dining room nicely decorated by everybody who had to be there for the holiday. It seemed to distract us from our sense of loss for being away from home. I sang along with everybody

官手上。他放下酒杯，步履顛狂地站在餐廳中央，朗聲說：

「我是革命軍人。」

大夥兒全笑彎了腰。是酒後的醉語吧！我們如是揣測，怕是喝了不少的。

「我必須服從命令，效忠國家。」

底下又是一陣雷動的歡聲。他低下頭，緊握麥克風的雙手竟微微顫動了起來，然後幾近喃喃自語地接著說：

「傍晚，我接到通知，我的母親在今天過世了。……」

石破天驚的宣布使全場陷入一片悚動的靜寂，微

else, trying to forget a promise I would never be able to fulfill in my life. When we were getting slightly drunk, the microphone was in a colonel's hand. He had been drinking and laughing more than anybody else. He put his glass down and staggered to the center of the dining hall. He announced, "I'm a revolutionary soldier!"

Everybody died laughing, thinking he was totally drunk. We guessed he had drunk a fair amount.

"I have to take orders and be loyal to my country," continued the colonel.

Everybody cheered again. He lowered his head. His hands were still holding the microphone but quivering. He almost murmured, "I was just told this evening that my mother passed away today."

The shocking announcement terrified and silenced the whole

醺的酒意頓消。他紅了眼，顫聲說：

「我不能提前離開闈場，我必須對我的工作負責到底。……前些年，我父親過世時，我也奉命遠在東京，無法及時趕回。我是個不孝子，但身為革命軍人，忠孝不能兩全，我只有……所以，今晚，我要唱一首很悲傷的歌。……」

數度哽咽後，一首痛徹心肺的悲愴旋律，斷斷續續流洩在燈火已闌的暗夜中，直到他掩面泣不成聲。啊！原來豪飲狂歡是另一種的至痛無言！而我，因著元宵燈會而刻意隱忍的傷痛亦早隨著止不住的淚水滂沱直下。去年燈會期間，適值父親北上就醫因跌斷而久不癒合的手腳，從窗口望去，中正紀念堂邊兒，人潮如織，香肩影動，笑語聲來，我四處商借一張輪椅不果後，曾和父親約定，次年必排除萬難，偕伊共賞如沸如撼的燈節盛會。而今，電視新聞中，中正紀念堂的燈籠高掛如列星，童玩技藝紛陳，觀賞的人潮簇

crowd. Everybody was now sober. He said with tearful eyes and a trembling voice, "I can't leave this place now. I have to be responsible for my work until it's done…A few years ago, when my father passed away, I was on duty in Tokyo. I couldn't go home for him, either. I'm not a filial son. But as a soldier, I have to choose between my country and my parents. I cannot but…So, tonight I'm going to sing a very sad song."

His song stuck in his throat a few times. Then the sad melody, covering deep grief, flew intermittently into the dark night until he couldn't help but end it with painful crying, covering his tearful face with his hands. I realized partying and drinking was just a way to cover up the pain, extreme beyond description. My pain, which I had tried to hide for the Lantern Festival celebration, was coming out in a flood of tears, too. Last Lantern Festival was when my father came to Taipei to seek better treatment for his broken arm and leg. Through a window, we saw a crowd near Chiang Kai-Shek Memorial Hall. It was a bustling and joyful scene. I had tried everything I could to borrow a wheelchair for my father, but I didn't get one. I promised my father that I would overcome any difficulty in order to take him to a boisterous and impressive

擁如《東京夢華錄》中的太平盛世，而父親卻已乘鶴遠去，骨肉乖隔，寧非人生之至痛？

那晚，我和淚躺下，衾枕盡溼，朦朧中入夢，卻是個以星月、煙花的璀璨始，以鮮血、眼淚的心碎終的夢魘。難道父親不避黃泉路迢遙，千里來入夢，真為奔赴這場生前未了的紅塵盛筵？

父親一生最喜熱鬧繁華。蒔花、養鳥、運動、旅行，把生活妝點得繽紛多彩。退休後，最喜歡拜訪朋友，最企盼兒女返家團聚。到後來，身體狀況已相當不佳時，還因扶杖掙扎著要去參加朋友的喪禮，而數度和母親反目。母親憐惜他身體孱弱，不願他奔波勞

Lantern Festival celebration next time. When this year's Lantern Festival at Chiang Kai-Shek Memorial Hall was on TV, I saw lanterns up high as stars, traditional handicrafts in eye-catching displays, and a crowd as delighted as people in the prosperous society described in the Chinese classic *Dreamy Splendor of the Eastern Capital.* But my father was gone as if he had flown away on a crane. I, who came from his flesh and blood, would never see him again. Isn't this the utmost pain of life?

That night I wept in bed, with my pillow and blanket all wet. I had a dream. It began with the splendor of the stars, the moon, and fireworks. But it ended with heartbreaking tears and blood as a nightmare. Did my father come all the way from another world into my dream, just for this festival he had wanted to attend?

My father enjoyed boisterous gatherings and splendid festivals all his life. He also liked to decorate life with hobbies such as gardening, bird keeping, sports, and traveling. After he retired, he loved to visit friends and looked forward to his children's every visit. Even when he was in poor health, he would struggle to go to a friend's funeral with a cane and argue with my mother, who

累，甚至見景傷情；他卻為不能親向朋友作最後的敬禮而懊惱。他憤恨地抱怨：

「死後才見交情。告別式上的熱鬧與否，可以看出這人做人有成功否。最後一面都不見，算什麼親戚朋友！」

他交代我們，把寄來的訃文一一登錄起來，他說：

「以後，我若是過身，你一定要記住寄一張白帖子倒轉去。」

迎著我們錯愕的眼光，他慢條斯理地解釋道：

「安捏卡鬧熱。告別式無人來，會給人恥笑，給人講我無人緣。我希望我的告別式可以鬧熱滾滾。像你屘叔的告別式，人山人海，看著極好哩，極讓人欣羨！免以為我的朋友死去，伊的後生就不會來，攏總給伊寄去，懂禮數的人就會來。」

was against the idea. My mother was afraid that going to a funeral would exhaust or even depress him. But he felt upset about not being able to pay the last tribute to his friends.He grudgingly complained, "It shows how good a friendship is, when the friend is dead. Whether one's funeral draws many people shows how popular this person is. If you don't even go to see this person for the last time, what kind of relative or friend are you?"

He told us to record all the funeral invitations he had received for him. He said, "Later, when I pass away, you must send funeral invitations to these people."

Seeing that we were astonished, he slowly explained, "That would make it boisterous. If nobody comes to my funeral, people will laugh at me and say I'm not popular. I hope my funeral will be as boisterous as your youngest uncle's, with crowds as big as a mountain or an ocean! His funeral looked great, very enviable! Don't think that my friends died and their children won't come. Just invite all of them. Those who know courtesy will come."

　　我故意別過臉去，不理他。我雖偶爾亦在課堂上和學生高談莊子曠達的生死觀，但面對父親這般赤裸裸地安頓自己的身後事，才知王羲之「固知一死生為虛誕，齊彭殤為妄作」真真道盡了世間兒女平凡的心事。高深豁達的哲理，只宜作學術的討論，小門深巷裡，椿萱康健才是真正的心願。

　　近年來，父親應是經常在思索著死生大事的。一回，他憂心忡忡地問我：

　　「人說死去以後，火葬比較卡清潔，你感覺安怎？未知會極痛否？」

　　我笑答：

　　「人死去，那會還有感覺！」

I purposefully turned away, not to reply to him. I had occasionally discussed Chuang-Tze's philosophy, which takes life and death lightly, with my students in class. But it was difficult to face my father's plainspoken attitude toward death. At that moment I realized what the ancient Chinese writer Wang His-chih meant when he said, "Everyone knows it is absurd to see life and death as one; it is fictitious to describe long life and early death as the same." That really expresses what's on everybody's mind. Profound and clairvoyant philosophy is only for intellectual discussion. To us ordinary people, what we really want is that our parents stay healthy in our small houses.

In recent years, my father often thought about his death. Once he asked me with great concerns, "People say it's cleaner to have the body cremated. What do you think? Does it hurt badly?"

I answered with a smile, "Who can feel pain after death?"

　　從那以後，他便四處去看存放骨灰的骨塔，並自己相中了一處，好幾次拉著我去看，都被我拒絕了。我氣他一直在為死亡做準備。

　　前年舊曆年，兄弟姊妹全回家。父親因夜半在浴室跌了一跤，手上正打著石膏，精神原本很差。見兒女們都回來，非常高興，吵著要去理髮，要到照相館去照相。我拿出相機，為他和家人合拍了些照片，他顯得神清氣爽，一直對著鏡頭微笑，我們直取笑他愈老愈會搶鏡頭。照完了相，我正捲著底片，他仍糾纏著母親一起去照相館，母親說：

　　「不是剛才照過了嗎？去照相館做啥米？」

　　他靦腆地說：

　　「你嘸知啦！你跟我去，咱拍一張合照，以後，我若死去，禮堂上才有一張卡好看的相片掛。」

Then he went to some pagodas keeping the ashes of the dead. He chose one of them and kept asking me to see it. But I turned him down altogether. I was angry at his preparation for death.

The year after that, during the Chinese New Year, I gathered with all my siblings at my parents' house. My father had fallen down in the bathroom at night and broken an arm. That arm was in a cast. He didn't have much energy until all of us came home. Then he was excited, talking about getting a haircut and having some pictures taken at a photo shop. I used my camera to take a few photos of him and the rest of the family. He looked energetic, constantly smiling at the camera. We made fun of him, saying he was more and more photogenic as he got older and older. When I finished a roll of film and began to rewind it, he still asked my mother to go to a photo shop with him. My mother said, "Didn't we just take pictures? What are we going to a photo shop for?"

He replied with an embarrassed look on his face, "You don't understand. You go with me. Let's have a picture taken together. Then when I die, there will be a very good-looking picture in the funeral hall."

　　我們聽了全傻了眼。母親一楞，隨即玩笑般的打圓場：

　　「你要掛在告別式上面，我才不要跟你合照，那有人在喪禮上掛合照，笑死人咧！」

　　他突然變得像個孩子似的，隔不了幾分鐘，又反反覆覆提起同樣的話頭，我耐下性子，像哄孩子似的說：

　　「你現在手上打著石膏，脖子上吊著繃帶，照起相來多難看，等你石膏拆下來，我再帶你去，好嗎？」

　　父親悵然若有所失，喃喃自語：
　　「再慢一下，就未赴啦！」

　　我佯裝嗔怪，質問：
　　「未赴做啥？不要亂講啦！」

We were all stunned. My mother paused and then jokingly said, "If you want it for the funeral, I'm not going to do it. Who has a picture of two people at one person's funeral? People would laugh at us."

He became like a child all of a sudden. Every few minutes he brought up the same subject. I tried to be patient, as if I had been talking to a child. I said, "Your arm is in a cast. There is a sling hanging down your neck. This will look bad in a picture. When your arm is not in a cast anymore, I'll take you to a photo shop, OK?"

My father seemed to have a sense of loss. He murmured to himself, "If we wait a while, it'll be too late."

I pretended to find his remark strange and inappropriate. I asked, "What'll be too late? Don't talk nonsense!"

他定定看著我，神情又恢復茫然，只不斷重複：

「你嘸知啦！正經會未赴啦……」

父親不幸而言中。直至過世以前，石膏一直未曾拆下，父親臨終前最後的影像終究未能如願留下。除此之外，一切都在父親掌握之中。

去年四月四日，父親在長期的病痛中解脫逝去。悲痛惶急，全家人手足無措，不知從何做起，慢慢尋思，才發現這些年來，在閒話家常中，父親早已循序漸進地對自己的後事一一做了安排，別說喪葬儀式，就連祭壇上的鮮花款式、擺設圖案，都已有了腹案。

他體貼我們工作忙碌，又不願孤獨地面對死亡，所以，選擇三月二十八日凌晨昏迷，直到去世，整整八天，全家大小因著國定假日及春假，得以晝夜不離

He fixed his eyes on me, then looked lost again. He kept repeating, "You don't understand. It's really going to be too late…"

Unfortunately he was right. His arm was in a cast until he passed away. He didn't get to fulfill his wish to leave his last image to the world. But except that, everything was in his control.

On April 4 of last year, my father, who had been tortured by chronic illness, escaped his misery. Saddened and shocked, my whole family didn't know what to do. Not until we calmed down did we realize over all these years my father had already arranged everything for his death and gradually let us know in casual remarks. Not to mention the formality of his funeral, even the flowers on the altar and other decorations of the funeral hall had been designed.

He didn't want to interrupt our busy work. But he didn't want to face death alone, either. That was why he chose to fall into a coma on the early morning of March 28th. From that day until he passed away, the whole family was off work because of National

地陪他走完人生最後的一程。

　　清明過後，天氣一直陰雨連綿，父親出殯前一日，突然轉晴。那一夜，我至靈堂清理葬儀社布置靈堂所剪下的殘花敗葉，在慘白的燈光下，猛一抬頭，驀然發現懸掛高處、俯視塵寰的父親放大照片，似乎閃過了一絲詭譎的笑容，那樣子像是正為著私心裡一樁未為人識破的計謀得逞而竊竊歡喜著。我丟下掃把，抬頭認真端詳著，照片一如本人，一副自信滿滿的樣子，彷彿這一切的悲歡離合全由他一手策動。不知為什麼，我突然想起父親打從我們小時候就一直喜歡重複說起的兩個耳熟能詳的諧音話及歇後語：

　　「老師搬過厝，冊（氣）都是冊（氣）。」

　　「牽狗犁田，可惡至極！」

　　我不知道，這兩句話是不是正說出了我當時的心

holidays and spring break. We surrounded him day and night for eight days. We accompanied him at the end of his journey.

After the Tomb-sweeping Day, the weather was constantly cloudy and rainy. But it suddenly let up a day before my father's burial. That night I went to the funeral hall to clean up withered flowers and dead leaves on the floor. In pale light I raised my head and found my father, looking down at the earth from high up in an enlarged photo, with a tinge of a smirk. He looked as if he was secretly happy about a scheme of his that nobody saw through. I threw the broom away and looked at him closely. His picture looked exactly like the person, showing a lot of confidence, as if this farewell had all been his plan. I didn't know why I suddenly thought of two puns and allegorical sayings my father liked to repeat in front of my siblings and me when we were small.

"Teachers have moved house and books (anger)[1] are everywhere."

"It is extremely abominable to have dogs till fields."

I didn't know if these two sayings happened to express how I felt

---

1.———In Taiwanese dialect, "books" and "anger" have identical pronunciation.

情。我神經質地趁著四下無人，拿起一旁準備給花補充水分的風霧器，往父親的笑臉上噴，照片太高了，風霧器的水花搆不上，我使勁兒的壓，踮起腳尖費力的噴，父親居高臨下，一逕兒笑著，依然自信滿滿的樣子。我好恨他獨自開了這麼大個玩笑，居然沒事先偷偷向我——他一向最鍾愛的小女兒透露半分。那位同我一樣——喜歡吹牛，卻經常穿幫；喜歡說笑話，又常常說不好的爸爸，他怎麼可以無端的拋下了我，牽狗犁田！

在四濺的水花中，往事歷歷，掠上心頭。我想起小時候通學，上下學都得行經父親上班的鄉公所旁。常常下課後，筋疲力竭，便轉進爸爸的辦公室，等他下班，用腳踏車送我回去。父親的同事，不拘老小，見了我必高聲大喊：

「嗨！天送兄，你那撒嬌女兒來了。」

at the moment. Seeing that nobody was around, I did something crazy, taking up a sprinkler for watering flowers and spraying water at my father's smiling face. His picture was too high up for the water to reach. I pressed the sprinkler very hard and raised myself on my toes. My father was up there, still smiling, still showing a lot of confidence. I hated him for playing such a big trick. He didn't even leak the secret to me, his youngest and favorite daughter! This guy, my father, liked to brag and joke just as I do. He was as bad at bragging and joking as I am, too. How could he leave me for no reason? This was really "having dogs till fields!"

In splashes of water, I saw many memories. When I was a girl, the town hall where my father worked was on my way home from school. I was usually tired after school and didn't want to walk all the way home. I went to my father's office, to wait for him to give me a ride home on his bike after work. When my father's colleagues, young or old, saw me, they always raised their voices to tell my father, "Hi, Tien-Soong, your little princess is here."

父親總是喜孜孜的迎上來，幫我提過沉重的書包。當時，我那身淺藍襯衫、深藍褶裙的臺中女中制服想是給父親帶來許多榮耀的，畢竟鄉下地方，能考上臺中一流的女中的，是鳳毛麟角。我每回去，他總是講話特別大聲，動作特別誇大，故意問我考試成績如何，而當時正值叛逆期的我，總是故意不讓他的虛榮得逞。父親是極珍愛我們父女同騎腳踏車，輾過長長的歸途的那段時光的，而我，其實手攬著父親清瘦的腰身，也為著有這麼位玉樹臨風般的父親而感到無限快樂。然而，我卻緊緊抓住父親掩飾不住的弱點，當他熱切的問我：

「明天，還來辦公室等我嗎？」

我總是矯情地拿喬，故作猶豫地說：
「不一定啦！明天再看看！」

當年那種對擁有父親全然的寵愛的自信滿滿的模樣，想來亦正是得自父親的遺傳吧！

My father would always come to me with a big smile and help me carry my heavy book bag. At that time, my Taichung Girls' High School uniform, a light blue shirt and a dark blue skirt, brought a lot of honor to my father. That was because very few girls in my hometown, a village, could get in the best girls' high school in Taichung City. So my father talked louder and moved more whenever I was in his office. He liked to ask me about my grades for his colleagues to hear. But I, a teenager in revolt then, never let him gratify his vanity. I knew my father cherished the time when I was on his bike on our long way home. I actually enjoyed it, too. I liked holding his narrow waist from behind on the bike and felt proud of my father's good shape. However, I liked to play with my father's weakness, which he couldn't hide. Whenever my father eagerly asked, "Are you coming to the office tomorrow?"

I would pretend to think about it and say, "I'm not sure. We'll see tomorrow."

I was so confident about having my father's heart. That confidence was inherited from him, too, wasn't it?

等我大學畢業後，開始做事賺錢，父親一直走在前頭引領我前進。當我還是助教時，他已向外宣稱女兒擔任講師，研究所剛畢業任講師，他馬上主動幫我升等為副教授，我一路追趕不及，有時也不免停在路邊喘息埋怨。然而，小時候愛臉的我，不也曾因父親初中的學歷不夠光彩，而幾度向同學們宣稱父親是高級中學畢業嗎？有一回，甚至差一點偽造文書，在學校發下的表格上父親的「職務」欄內，主動為他升級為「課長」，只為嫌棄小小「課員」，在同學間擁有顯赫頭銜的爸爸群裡，實在太過寒磣。二十多年的歲月飛逝，昔日看不破虛名的小女兒在水深浪闊的十里紅塵中翻滾浮沉過後，已逐漸領悟素樸澹定的丰采，反倒踽步蹣跚的老父卻回首眺望繁華虛幻的海市蜃樓。

風霧器裡，終於再也擠壓不出任何水花。我頹然放下，跌坐在祭壇前的泥地上，和父親四目相視。人

After I finished college and began working, my father always led me to move up. When I was only a teaching assistant, he told everybody I was an instructor. When I finished graduate school and became an instructor, he said I was an associate professor. I had to catch up. Sometimes I stopped to take a break and complained about how he pressured me to get ahead. However, didn't I do something similar when I was a child sensitive to reputation? I thought my father's middle school diploma was not good enough and told my classmates he graduated from high school. Once I almost committed forgery. Instead of my father's real position "clerk" I wrote "supervisor" as his job title in a school form I had to fill out, just because I thought a "clerk" couldn't compare with my classmates' successful fathers. More than twenty years passed. That little girl who once couldn't see through the emptiness of fame went through waves of hardships and gradually understood the beauty of simplicity. But the father who tottered lonely through the years, on the contrary, looked back on life's journey and still thought of success like a desert traveler mistaking a mirage for an oasis.

No more water came out of the sprinkler in my hand. I disappointedly put it down and sat on the cement floor before the

人都說兄弟姊妹中，我長得最像父親，長臉孔、挺鼻梁、薄嘴脣、尖下巴，他們看到的是容貌，我知道的卻是看不見的心思，自小我便是父親如影隨形的小跟班。如今，形之不存，影將安附？

次日，豔陽高照，親戚朋友一大早便陸續湧至，旅居日本的堂哥、堂嫂更從大阪匍匐奔回。我們沒有遵照政府革新的指示，我們發了好多訃文出去，邀請所有認識父親的親朋好友前來，父親要一一同他們告別，父親多年來一直期盼的「鬧熱滾滾」的告別式，果真實現了。

我們披麻帶孝，跪倒在祭壇前，模糊的淚眼中，是一雙雙前來拈香的朋友的雙足，穿晶亮皮鞋的、高跟鞋的、布鞋的、趿著拖鞋的，甚至還有拄杖跟蹌而來的，從不同的鞋樣上看出了行業和身分，也看出了父親廣闊的交遊。我不停地一一叩首答拜，打從心裡

altar, looking up into my father's eyes. Everybody says I look more like my father than any of my siblings do. I have his long face, prominent nose, thin lips, and pointed chin. They only see the looks. But I know something connecting my father and me that can't be seen. I used to follow my father everywhere like a shadow. Now the body is gone. To what can the shadow attach itself?

The sun shone beautifully on my father's burial day. In the early morning, relatives and friends came in crowds. Even my cousin and his wife who lived in Osaka, Japan made the trip for the ceremony. My siblings and I didn't follow the government's campaign for simple funerals. We sent out many invitations, asking everybody who knew our father to come. Our father wanted to say good-bye to all of them. His wish for a "boisterous" funeral came true.

My siblings and I were in white linen robes, traditional funeral attire for the deceased's children. We were on our knees with lowered heads in front of the altar. Through our tears, we only saw the feet of those who came up with incense in hand to give blessings to our father. Some of those feet were wearing shiny leather shoes, others on heels, in running shoes, or in slippers.

感謝他們的深情厚意成全了父親最後的心願，讓他無憾地在人生途程中打上一個圓滿的休止符。

屬於父親的繁華終於散盡。熊熊烈火中，父親的肉身漸次消蝕殆盡，從小小玻璃窗內看去，我不禁全身悚慄，淚下如雨，父親一直是那麼個忍不住疼痛的人，烈火焚身，對他而言，是何等酷烈的煎熬。骨灰從火葬爐內推出時，照管火葬的先生特別叮囑，勿將淚水滴進骨灰中，我擦乾了淚，小心翼翼地用夾子夾起一塊父親的頭蓋骨放進罈內，心疼地在心裡重複千百遍父親曾經問過我的：

「會極痛苦？爸爸。」

父親逝世，至今已屆周年。這些日子來，我回想起他逝世前半年那段跌斷手腳的日子，總是深自責備

There were even staggering feet with a cane. Different footwear showed different occupations and social statuses, which indicated my father had made friends with people from all walks of life. I bowed to them one by one and thanked them from the bottom of my heart for their loving thoughts to fulfill my father's last wish, to put a perfect end to the journey of his life.

All the splendor about my father came to an end. His body was disappearing in a burning fire. I looked into the small window of the crematorium and shuttered with tears falling like rain. My father never took pain very well. How cruel it must have been for him to go through cremation. When the ashes were pushed out of the crematorium, a man in charge of the crematorium told my family and me not to drop tears into the ashes. I wiped my tears, carefully picked up a piece of my father's skull, and put it in an earthen jar. With an aching heart, I whispered "Dad" and repeated thousands of times what my father had once asked me, "Does it hurt badly?"

My father has been gone for a year. All this time I have been thinking about the last six months of his life. I can't feel more

沒能為父親付出更多的耐心和寬容。父親一向極畏疼痛，稍有病痛，常極盡呻吟之能事，以致後來真正病痛難忍，我們都懷疑他只是裝腔作勢。他夜半如廁，摔倒於洗手間內，我們一直為他延請骨科大夫診治，孰知，慢性腦溢血才是癥結所在。從臨終前所照X光片看來，醫生斷定他體內出血已非一朝半日。因為腦部神經為逐漸滲出且凝結的血塊所擠壓，因此，在那半年內，他的神智時而清醒一如常人，時而迷糊健忘得教人吃驚，然而，因為他平日喜歡開玩笑，我們一直以為他在裝瘋賣傻。一日黃昏，他居然坐在沙發上指著在陽臺修剪花木的外子，悄聲問母親：

「那人是誰？」

母親初始不以為意，答：

「是我們女婿啊！」

guilty about not having more patience and lenience with him then, when he suffered from broken bones. My father hated pain. He whined more than anybody would whenever he was a little ill. That was why my family and I thought he was exaggerating when he was actually in unbearable pain. After he broke his arm and leg by falling down in the bathroom late at night, we took him to see an orthopedist. We didn't know internal bleeding in his head was the real problem. A doctor judged by an X-ray my father took right before his death that he had been bleeding inside for quite a while. His brain nerves were pressured by blood clots from time to time. No wonder he was surprisingly forgetful sometimes in his last six months, though he appeared to be normal at times as well. Little did we know. We thought he was faking a loss of memory as a joke, because he liked joking. Sitting on a sofa one evening, he pointed at my husband, who was trimming plants on the balcony, and asked my mother, "Who's that guy?"

My mother didn't take it seriously. She replied, "He's our son-in-law."

他似乎有些納悶，搔著頭說：

「那我們的女兒又是誰啊？」

母親不悅地說：

「到底是真的，還是假的。你免嚇驚我。」

我一點也沒拿他這番話當真的，我趨向前，傍著他坐下，推擠他，笑說：

「好會假仙哦！假得還真像！好！那你說，如果我不是你女兒，你倒說說看，我是誰？」

他習慣性的聳聳肩，似乎被我說得有些不好意思，這件事就這般真假莫辨地過去。

除了迷糊健忘外，其後，他還逐漸變得脾氣古怪不馴。那段時間內，母親自然是吃盡了苦頭的。白天情況尚不難應付，每到夜晚，便頻頻框喝，一下子要人攙扶他上洗手間，一會兒又要人倒水，再不就繞室

He seemed puzzled. He scratched his head and asked, "Who's our daughter then?"

My mother was displeased. She frowned and said, "Are you faking? Don't scare me."

I didn't think he meant it. I approached and sat beside him, pushed him lightly, and said with a smile, "You really know how to put one over. It seemed real! Ok, tell me, if I am not your daughter, who am I?"

he shrugged as he usually did. He seemed embarrassed by me. This incident passed without being clarified.

He was not only forgetful but gradually became irritable. My mother suffered a great deal during that time. He was all right during the day, but very demanding at night. He would ask my mother to take him to the bathroom, to pour water for him, to do endless things. Or he would walk around the bedroom all night

徘徊，彷彿床上藏了什麼妖魔鬼怪，硬是不肯躺下安歇，母親被折騰得幾乎崩潰，父親偏又不肯讓兒女代勞。

元宵節他北上就醫，住我處，一連七天，夜半不眠，每隔三分鐘，便要母親攙扶起床，我在隔室，聽見他呼天搶地，心裡大慟。一夜，我實在忍不住了，強迫母親至他房歇息，由我全權照料，父親以頭撞牆，誓死反對，口裡直喊：

「我會死啊，我會死啊……你們實在可惡至極啊……」

闃寂的暗夜中，一聲比一聲淒厲，然後，開始一反常態地破口大罵母親無情，母親聞言，淚潸然直下，我忍不住厲聲責備他：

「你再罵，小心媽媽從此不理會你。你把媽媽整垮了，以後，看誰有她那樣的耐性來照顧你！」

and wouldn't go to bed, as if there had been a monster hiding in bed. My mother almost collapsed. But my father wouldn't let us children replace her to take care of him.

That Lantern Festival he was staying at my place because he had come to Taipei to see a doctor. During the visit, seven nights in a row he wouldn't sleep. He asked my mother to help him get up every three minutes. I was in the next room and heard his screaming. I was shattered. One night I couldn't hold it back anymore. I forced my mother to sleep in another room and took over her duties to look after my father. My father opposed the decision. He banged his head against a wall and cried, "I'll die! I'll die! You guys are despicable!"

His screams were more and more piercing in the quiet night. Then he began to call my mother cold-blooded, totally unlike the way he usually was. My mother burst into tears. I couldn't help scolding him, "If you continue blaming Mom, she won't talk to you anymore. If you make her collapse, who's going to take care of you with her kind of patience?"

他似是豁出去的態勢，狠話拚命出籠：

「我才無稀罕，才不用你們來照顧。……」

我軟硬兼施，滿頭大汗；他負嵎頑抗，像負傷的野獸，直到天濛濛亮，才倦極睡去。我見他蜷曲酣睡如稚子的容顏，真是欲哭無淚。

那日中午，他悠悠醒來，我攙扶他至客廳坐下，他笑語如常，我婉陳他昨日之非，他茫昧不復記省，只頻頻否認：

「那有這款代誌！我那會安捏無良心！騙肖仔！……」

經眾人舉證歷歷後，他似乎也被自己異常的行為所震懾。沉默不語良久後，他背著母親，低聲附耳和我說：

「敢真有安捏？如果真有這款代誌，實在太不是

It seemed that he could not care less. He kept saying harsh words and declared, "I don't care. I don't need you guys to take care of me!"

I tried everything I could. I was sweating. He struggled desperately like a wounded animal. Finally he fell asleep at dawn. I looked at his childlike expression in deep sleep. I wanted to cry but had no more tears.

He woke up leisurely at noon. I helped him walk to the living room and sit down. He talked and joked as usual. I told him what he had done in a mellow way. He didn't seem to remember. He denied it, "How could that have happened? How could I have been so mean? You are lying!"

When other witnesses supported what I said, he seemed shocked by his own strange behavior the night before. After a long silence, he whispered into my ear behind my mother, "Did I really do that? If it really happened, it's too ridiculous. Please apologize to your mom for me, OK? Or she won't talk to me."

款咧。……拜託你給你老母會失禮一下，好嗎？要
不，伊會不肯理我……」

　　那時，我是如此地無知，錯以為他返老還童，故
意虛張聲勢以博取憐惜。事後追憶起來，也許，父親
視平躺如畏途，正是腦血四溢，痛苦不堪的生理反應
也未可知，然而，做為女兒的我，是以何等的不耐來
照看父親無法言宣的痛楚呢？這世界何其荒謬，何以
最深沉的反省，常只能在無法彌補的悔恨之後？

　　這些天，我一直翻閱著昔時的照片，在一本本的
相簿中，父親一逕地以他招牌的笑容光燦地面對鏡
頭。從年輕到年老，從紅顏到白髮，從山巔到海隅，
從打球到下棋，從加州的水綠沙暄，到北海道的冰雪
滿地，從人子到人父，甚至人祖……他總是那般興高
采烈地擁抱生活。生命中的繁華，原不論高堂華筵或
淺斟低酌的，父親的一生，充滿了小市民知足強韌的

At that time I was so ignorant I thought he was acting like a child and bluffing purposefully to curry favor. Now I look back on it. He hated lying down probably because blood was oozing in his head and causing unbearable pain. But I, his daughter, had so little patience with his unspoken suffering! This world is absurd. Why does the deepest reflection only come after you regret something for which you can never compensate?

These days I keep looking through old photo albums. My father always appears in the pictures with his unique brilliant smile, from ruddy youth to golden years, from mountaintop to seashore, from a ball game to a chess game, from greenish water and warm sand in California to a winter snow in Japan. He cheerfully embraced life all the time, no matter as a son, a father, or a grandfather. The splendor of life doesn't discriminate. An average Joe can have it as much as the rich enjoy their feast. My father's life was the gorgeous epitome of an ordinary person's contentment and strength. It was

迤邐華彩，繽紛熱鬧。我有幸與他結下四十餘年的父女緣，陪他在人生舞臺上賣力淋漓地演出一場，如今，曲終人散，留在心底的，豈只是止不住的悲傷！

——原載一九九二年五月十三日《中國時報》

收入九歌版《不信溫柔喚不回》（2006年）

colorful and flamboyant. I was fortunate to perform dedicatedly with him on the stage of life as his daughter for over forty years. Now the play came to an end and the audience disappeared. What he left me has been more than endless sorrow at the bottom of my heart.

"The Chinese PEN" **Winter, 2000**

年過五十
Life After Fifty

胡守芳／譯

Translated by Shou-Fang HU-MOORE

年過五十，雖不至於萬念俱灰，卻真是心如止水。再沒有小鹿亂撞的激情，只有笑看、旁觀的怡然。人生諸多情緣俱皆化為涓涓流水，既無過不去的敵人，自然也談不上莫逆，真誠服膺所謂的「君子之交淡如水」！對美麗有幾近病態的喜愛，對醜陋卻也無所謂能不能忍受。年過五十，完全明白人生無法求全的缺憾，逐漸能易位思考，對荒謬微笑、和遺憾握手！

年過五十的心情，真是百味雜陳，說也說不清。

黃昏時分，我日日踞坐電腦桌前，將自己童稚、少年及中年的光燦笑容一一掃描進蘋果電腦裡，夕陽在護目鏡裡一點一點沉落，電腦螢幕的深處，反射出一張既悵惘又失落的面容。Photoshop裡的橡皮擦，除去了照片裡伊人的皺紋，卻抹不去現實人生中的黑瘢。樂觀竟然和失眠共存！失眠居然和發胖比肩，發胖奇異地與皺紋共生，皺紋又弔詭地和慈眉善目如影隨形！……五十歲後的女人，就是以這樣光怪陸離的矛盾，遲緩而乏力地和歲月拔河，且注定向老邁一路傾斜過去，無論周遭的人如何信誓旦旦地稱讚你看起來依然年輕。

年過半百後，心境有了奇妙的轉變。許多以往錙銖必較的，如今漫不經心，譬如友誼或愛情；有些昔

My feelings about passing the age of fifty are so variegated that it is difficult to put them into words.
Day after day at dusk I sit in front of the computer desk scanning one by one the bright smiles of my childhood, youth, and middle age into the Apple computer. The setting sun sinks slowly in my protective glasses and in the deep of the computer monitor a gloomy and bewildered face is mirrored. The eraser function of Photoshop wipes out wrinkles on the face of the person in the photos, but cannot obliterate the blotches of real life. Optimism, to my surprise, actually co-exists with insomnia! Insomnia can actually be closely correlated with gaining weight. Weight strangely increases together with wrinkles. And wrinkles ironically accompany a benign face. Faced with all these bizarre contradictions, a woman after fifty sluggishly and powerlessly plays a tug-of-war with time and is destined to lean all the way through the aging process, regardless of how people around her solemnly swear that she still looks very young.

After fifty, one's state of mind takes an intriguing turn. Many issues over which one used to haggle meticulously in the past become negligible now, such as friendship or love. Some matters

日滿不在乎的，現在觸目驚心，譬如皺紋或贅肉。改考卷時，最痛恨學生在文章裡動輒稱呼「五十老嫗」「半百老翁」，看電視時，最討厭主播不時重播獨居老人萎死家中、多日無人聞問的畫面。十八歲的時候，曾經因為厭惡年老色衰，發誓絕不苟活，決定只要年過三十，即刻引火自焚或切腹自盡，效法日本武士道精神，留下雖然未必燦爛卻仍舊富於青春的容顏。所以，三十歲過得最久、最纏綿，一直捨不得鬆口，忝顏延長到接近三十又五，才悻悻然改口道：「燦爛不必一定年輕，成熟往往更具風韻」；四十歲後，還能和親朋笑談肌肉日漸鬆弛、記憶逐漸模糊；五十過後，明顯開始避談與衰老相關話題，只一味向人展示歸納分析能力！可心底老不安寧，明明自幼就丟三落四，現在只要一找東西，便慌張地以為老年痴呆症忽焉來臨。

of which one could care less in the old days become alarmingly disturbing now, such as wrinkles or excessive fat. While marking exam papers, what I hate most is seeing the random use of "an old woman of fifty" or "a man half a century old" in students' essays. While watching television, what I resent most is the re-broadcast of scenes regarding a lonely old man who has been dead in his house for days without anyone knowing. At the age of eighteen, I once swore not to live long because of my disgust at the loss of beauty in old age. I decided that once reaching thirty I would immediately commit self-immolation or hara-kiri, following the spirit of Japanese bushido, in order to keep my still youthful, though not necessarily glamorous, looks. For this reason, I had the most prolonged and sentimental thirty, unwilling to part with it. It was not until approaching thirty-five that I changed my tune indignantly, "Glamour does not only belong to youth; maturity often has more charm." After forty, I was still able to have laughing conversations with friends and relatives about the gradually flabby muscles and blurring memories. After passing fifty, I have clearly started to avoid topics having to do with old age and simply insist on showing off my inductive and analytical abilities. However, there is a constant uneasiness in my heart. Although I have always had a

年過半百，心腸變得像鋼鐵一樣堅硬，卻又易碎如透明的水晶。生命裡的原則大體底定，固然不大願意接受委屈，也從未想到占便宜。以往，每到暑假，總和一干成績被當的學生纏綿悱惻。這些年，再沒有做過到教務會議去承認分數計算錯誤以拯救出局學生的行徑。吃了秤鉈鐵了心！視學生提前出局為另類轉型。雖然沒有以關機或拒接電話來杜絕求情，但是，凡來關說者，我一律跳脫攸關分數的所有黏纏辯證，立刻轉移焦點，逕自切入「危機即是轉機」的勸勉，絕不讓對方有可乘之機。然而，嚴詞拒絕過後，一想到家長的焦慮、學生的悔恨，心裡往往糾結拉扯，不是食不下嚥，就是在暗夜裡睜眼到天明。生活裡小小的溫情，經常被擴大為了不得的善意；人際間的扞格，又常常被縮小成無意間的擦槍走火。學生情感受

habit of losing things since childhood, I now nervously suspect the sudden onset of Alzheimer every time I look for something.

After age fifty, one's heart becomes as hard as steel, yet at the same time as brittle as transparent crystal. The principles of life are mostly established. Although one is not willing to be treated unfairly, neither has one contemplated taking advantage of others. At summer breaks in the past, I used to feel sorry for the students who couldn't get a passing grade. But, in recent years, I no longer attend the meetings of student affairs to rescue these students by declaring a miscalculation of their marks. I have steeled my heart and regard the earlier discharge of these students as an alternative direction for their future. Although I do not cut off students' pleas by unplugging or refusing to answer the phone, I have freed myself from all the tangled arguments over marks and immediately shift the focus by encouraging them to turn crisis into opportunity so as to not provide any avenue for exploitation. However, after the stern refusal, whenever I think about the worries of parents and the regrets of students, my heart often becomes so entangled that I lose either appetite or sleep. A little warmth in life is often magnified to be the greatest kindness, while interpersonal conflicts

挫，紅著眼眶到研究室來尋求援助時，我的眼淚總是多過自來水，非但無法善盡開導的重責，還哭得比學生更傷心！到頭來，甚至還得勞煩學生反過來安慰、輔導，並賭咒、發誓一定莊敬自強，請老師切莫淚淋淋！

年過五十，了然個體獨立的理論，夸夸宣言不再干涉兒女的行動，刻意維持開放、開明的假象，卻在兒女遲歸時，焦慮得差點兒撞牆！在他們考不上大學時幾乎抓狂！這時，才恍然大悟人們以「婆婆媽媽」來形容瑣碎囉唆的行徑，並非刻意汙衊女性，的確是其來有自。原本溫柔優雅的女性，年過五十，還能維持從容身段者幾希！養兒不再防老，養兒的最大功效，在培養大人動心忍性。五十歲的女人多半擁有業已成年、卻依然幼稚的兒女，這種可大、可小的彈性，被孩子們耍弄得淋漓盡致！當不肯接受約束

are often reduced to unintended accidents. When a student who is emotionally hurt comes to my office with red eyes seeking support, my tears always flow more copiously than tap water. I am not only unable to fulfill my duty in providing counsel but also become more inconsolable than the student. In the end the student has to be the one consoling and supporting me, while solemnly promising to be strong and self-uplifting so that I won't cry any more.

After fifty, one completely understands the theories of individual independence and boastfully declares non-interference with the activities of one's children, intentionally keeping a false facade of open-mindedness. Yet, whenever the children are home late, one is beside oneself with worries and nearly goes mad should they fail the university entrance exam. Only at this time does one suddenly realize that the expression "grannies and moms" used to describe mawkish and nagging behaviors is not intended to insult women, but merely derived from experience. Very few women who used to be gentle and graceful can still maintain the same composure after fifty. To raise children is no longer for the security of old age. Its chief function is to cultivate parental self-restraint and endurance. Most women at fifty have children who have already

時，他們會即刻搬出民法中的「成年」定義來爭取自由；需要金錢資助時，卻又馬上降回依人小鳥，口口聲聲親情無價、母愛至上，揭櫫同舟絕對必須共濟！父母和兒女兩造交鋒，最容易見證台灣民主開放教育的成效。兒女伶俐、便給的口齒和父母夾纏、矛盾的邏輯，恰恰是五十歲母親情緒崩潰的元凶，也是民主進步的見證。五十歲的女人成天在斷絕母子關係和修葺親情間苦苦掙扎！花最多時間在賭咒、發誓和悔恨上，轉眼卻又被兒女不經意的甜蜜輕易收服。

年過五十，雖不至於萬念俱灰，卻真是心如止水。再沒有小鹿亂撞的激情，只有笑看、旁觀的怡

reached adulthood yet behave like children. This adaptability to be either old or young is exploited by the children to the fullest extent. When they are not willing to submit to restraint, they will immediately use the definition of "adult" in civil law to strive for their freedom. Yet, when they need financial assistance, they immediately become as lovely and agreeable as little song birds, praising parental love as invaluable and maternal love as supreme, as well as proclaiming that people in the same boat should absolutely support each other. The battle between parents and children bears best witness to the effect to Taiwan's democratic open education. The eloquence of the children versus the self-contradictory logic of the parents is exactly the culprit that causes emotional breakdown in the fifty-year-old mother and as well, testimony to the progress of democracy. A woman at fifty struggles arduously all day long between the pendulum of cutting off the mother-child relationship and rebuilding parental devotion. She spends a lot of time cursing, swearing and repenting, yet can be easily pacified in an instant by the fortuitous sweetness of her children.

Once passing fifty, even though one may not go so far as to give up all ambitions and hopes, one's heart is truly like still water. There

然。人生諸多情緣俱皆化為涓涓流水，既無過不去的敵人，自然也談不上莫逆，真誠服膺所謂的「君子之交淡如水」！對美麗有幾近病態的喜愛，對醜陋卻也無所謂能不能忍受。年過五十，完全明白人生無法求全的缺憾，逐漸能易位思考，對荒謬微笑、和遺憾握手！以往，自認聰慧靈敏、身手矯捷，總想不明白，何以開車行經收費站，十有九次，怎麼先生老選擇最長的隊伍等候！忍不住建議他見縫插針，改變跑道；而他一貫我行我素，擇一而棲，不肯輕易更換。他的理由是：

「橫豎總會輪到，選擇了，便得安心鵠候，不要三心二意。否則，臨時更換跑道，擾亂了行車的秩序不說，還得擔負相當的風險。」

對這樣的說詞，我一貫嗤之以鼻，以為虛詞詭辯，不過是為反應遲鈍找藉口罷了！歲月無聲流去，

are no more passionate feelings that can cause irrational palpitations. There is only the pleasant contentment of a smiling observer. All the emotional attachments in life have become as calm as a brook. One has neither mortal enemies nor bosom friends, truly following the Confucian teaching to keep friendship as plain as water. One takes an almost morbid liking for beauty, yet neither is there any intolerance for ugliness. A woman after fifty completely understands that life is not perfect and is gradually able to change her way of thinking, to smile at absurdity as well as to make peace with regrets. In the past, I used to regard myself mentally intelligent and physically agile and could never understand why my husband always chose the longest line at the toll station nine times out of ten. I couldn't help suggesting that he should seek an opportunity to switch lanes, but he always unswervingly remained in the lane he had chosen, unwilling to change. His reason was: "Sooner or later it will be our turn. Once you choose a line, stay in it without worrying. Don't shilly-shally. Otherwise, by changing lanes at the spur of the moment, you will not only disturb the traffic order but will also take a big risk."

I used to always snigger at his reasoning, thinking he was simply using sophistry to make an excuse for his slow reaction. As

他一逕慢條斯理，個性躁急的我卻在移動的光陰中逐漸領略了不疾不徐、按部就班的不易。一日，在收費站前的長龍中，忽然頓悟，丈夫不肯更換跑道原來是一項值得稱頌再三的德行，否則以我的暴烈、懶惰與苟且習性，若另一半缺少耐性，怕早就連夜潛逃無蹤，細數起來，收費站前的車陣哪有我的缺點來得多！

年過半百，對個人的要求越來越多，對公義的追求卻越來越熱烈。因為知道人性的脆弱，所以，對別人逐漸有了同情的理解；也因為洞悉人性的弱點，理解沒有了制度，難以規範人心，所以，對社會的制度及公義越發求全。年少時的獨善其身，有了「姑息養奸」的新解，威權體制下被壓抑的情緒，隨著閱歷的增長悄悄蓄積成爆發力十足的多管閒事：投書、打電話抗議、貼海報、寫文章論辯……就只差沒綁白布

time passes without a sound and he carries on in his unhurried manner, I have, however, gradually come to appreciate how hard it is to take the time of doing things in good order. One day in a long line in front of the tollbooth, I suddenly realized that my husband's unwillingness to switch lanes is actually a virtue to be applauded. Otherwise, were it not for his patience in dealing with my hot temper, laziness and perfunctory nature, he probably would have run away without a trace in the middle of the night. My shortcomings added together are probably more numerous than the cars lining up in front of the toll station.

After fifty, one has less and less personal demands, yet one's pursuit of justice becomes more and more feverish. Because of knowledge about human frailty, one gradually develops more compassionate understanding towards others. At the same time, with more insight into human weakness, one realizes it will be difficult to make people conform to rules, if there is no institution in place. Therefore, one starts to demand more social structure and justice. In my youth I only asked myself to behave virtuously, which I now regard as tolerating evil. The emotions suppressed under the authoritarian rule have quietly built up as my experience

條上街頭抗爭，熱血奔騰、桀傲不馴強過青春期的少年！

年過半百後，忽然萌生前所未有的好奇心與求知慾，推開保守、摒棄成見，銳意和新世界接軌！不認輸地追趕新資訊，頑強地和日益消退的腦力抗爭！我低聲下氣向女兒請益，只為操作電腦軟體；孜孜向學生叩問，只是不願被時代遠遠拋棄！我勇敢嘗試上網教學，讓鍵盤替代黑板、螢光幕取代教室；利用最新電腦科技，以文字和圖片儲存最最古老的記憶。我像海綿一樣，急急吸水，哪管水源來自何方！然而，匍匐前行之際，畢竟還是難免頻頻回顧。吐納之時，雖偶露疲態，顯得氣喘吁吁，卻不改顧盼自雄、旁若無人，完全不去想人生伊於胡底。

grows. Eventually it explodes into minding others' business, such as sending letters to the newspaper, protesting by phone, putting up posters, writing articles to debate and so forth, just short of attending a street protest with a white ribbon tied around my head. My boiling passion and unruliness is even stronger than that of a teenager.

After fifty, one has a sudden surge of curiosity and craving for knowledge. Pushing away conservastism and abandoning bias, one is determined to get connected with the new world. One pursues new information unyieldingly and fights tenaciously against deteriorating brainpower. In order to operate computer software, I modestly ask my children for help. I beseech my students' advice diligently, simply because I don't want to be left behind as time advances. I bravely try my hand at on-line teaching, letting the keyboard replace the blackboard and the monitor the classroom. I use the most advanced computer technology to store the most ancient memories in the word and picture files. I desperately absorb knowledge like a sponge absorbing water regardless of the water source. However, in the process of crawling forward, I still cannot help looking backwards constantly. Although once in a while I may appear tired and seem to be gasping for air, I still carry on with

　　年過五十，以平均年齡分析，生命已向頹勢逐漸歪斜。以人生歷練歸納，智慧經驗正臻高地。五十歲，說老，不算太老；說年輕，可不年輕！以往在筵席，總是敬陪末座，如今步步高升，距離首席不到幾張椅。負責俛首稱是的時代已然過去，最新任務是絞盡腦汁開闢話題。生活的重心逐漸由情感的斟酌轉移到器官的救濟。一桌子吃飯，總有不識相的人開始為你計算卡路里；當你體態略顯豐腴，即刻有人建議你到健身俱樂部去鍛鍊身體；當你步履稍微蹣跚，立即有人提醒你應該及時休息。可我才不甘心老在這未老先衰的議題裡打轉，春陽和煦、夏日鷹揚、秋高氣爽、冬月映雪，四季各有其輝煌燦爛，若放眼不見繁花盛景，豎耳聽不到鶯啼燕囀，開口只道八卦短長，如何能跟蘇東坡一樣，在晴時多雲偶陣雨的人生風雨中，從容地策杖吟嘯徐行！

cocksure composure, not brothering to think what life is about.

Surveying the average life span of human being shows that the portion after fifty is spent leaning downhill. But by summing up life's experience, one's wisdom level has reached a higher ground. The age fifty is neither old nor young. Attending banquets in the past, I used to always sit in an inconspicuous seat. Now my seat gradually moves forward to just a few from the head table. The age of nodding submissively has gone and the newest responsibility now is to cudgel one's brains into expanding the topics of conversation. The center of gravity in life has gradually shifted from contemplating emotional matters to preserving one's organs. At the dining table there is always somebody who is audacious enough to start calculating your calories. When your physique appears to be a bit plump, someone will immediately suggest that you should go to a fitness center for exercise. When your step seems to limp slightly, someone will immediately remind you to take a rest. But I am not willing to go round and round on the topics of premature aging. The spring sun is warm, while the summer sun soars. Autumn has crisp and clear air, while the winter moon reflects its light on the snow. Every season has splendor all its own. If one does not open

　　年過五十，雖然越來越貪生怕死，卻從未認真從事攸關延長壽命的任何活動，五穀依舊不分、四體越發不勤。飯桌上，絕不煞風景地拒絕肥碩欲滴的蹄膀；平日喝咖啡像倒開水，電腦桌前一坐便是大半天。乾眼症跟著五十肩，胃痛加上失眠，我都視之為天將降大任的考驗。啊！年過半百，其實已胸無大志，一點也不想兼善天下，既沒有本事做大官，也不想聽國父的話去做大事，只偷偷祈求一點點的榮華，一些些的富貴，少少的美貌和一位跑不掉的丈夫。

　　　　　　　　　——選自二魚版《五十歲的公主》（2002年）

the eyes to see beautiful scenes of blossoms, nor hear the birds singing, but rather wastes time on gossip, how can one be like the ancient poet Su Tung-po[1] who walked leisurely with a cane reciting poems while weathering unsettled storms throughout his life?

After age fifty, even though clinging onto life more and more cravenly, one has not seriously taken actions to prolong one's life. Like an old-style intellectual, I still have difficulty telling the five grains apart, and my limbs move less and less. At the dining table, I simply won't spoil the fun by refusing to eat the greasy dish of pork leg. I pour down coffee like water everyday and sit in front of the computer all day long. Dry-eye syndrome, frozen shoulders, stomach ache and insomnia are all regarded by me as God's testing. Alas, after age fifty, I have in fact lost all ambitions; neither have I any wish to see the world saved. I have no ability to acquire a high position in government, nor any desire to follow Dr. Sun Yat-sen's teaching of doing great things for society. I only secretly pray for a little bit of fame and fortune, some beauty, as well as a husband who will not run away from me.

"The Chinese PEN" Spring, 2005

1.———*Su Tung-po (1037-1101), famous poet and essayist in the Sung Oynasty.*

如果記憶像風
If Memories Were Like the Wind

湯麗明／譯

Translated by Li-Ming Tang

那些施暴的孩子的行徑，著實可用「可恨」或「可惡」來形容，我必須慚愧的承認，如果我早知道那些孩子是如此殘忍地對待我的女兒！我是絕不會那樣委曲求全地去和行凶者打交道的，我也深信，沒有任何一個母親會加以容忍的，我是多麼對不起女兒呀！

我的女兒上國中，除了學校課業不甚理想外，她開朗、乖巧、體貼且善解人意，

我們雖然偶爾在思及「優勝劣敗」的慘烈升學殺伐時，略微有些擔心外，整體而言，我們對她相當滿意，尤其在聽到許多同輩談及他們的女兒如何成天如刺蝟般地和父母唱反調、鬧彆扭時，外子和我都不禁暗自慶幸。

去年暑假，考高中的兒子從學校領回了聯考成績單，母子倆正拿著報紙上登載的分數統計表，緊張地核算著可能考上的學校，女兒從學校的暑假輔導課放學，朝我們說：

「事情爆發了！」

女兒每天放學總是一放下書包便跟前跟後的和我報告學校見聞，相干的，不相干的。這時候，大夥兒

As a student in junior high school, my daughter's academic performance was mediocre, but she had a sweet personality—cheerful, charming, tender and considerate.

We were perfectly happy with her, though once in a while, our thoughts might have been overshadowed by the prospect of her struggling in the relentless exam-oriented educational system where only the fittest survive. When our friends talked about how their daughters threw tantrums or were forever at odds with them, we were thankful that our daughter was different.

Last year, during the summer vacation, my son, who was hoping to enter high school, came back home one day with his entrance exam results, forwarded to him through his old school. While we were nervously matching his scores against the basic requirements of individual high schools, my daughter came back from her summer school.

"All hell has broken loose!" she shouted in our direction.

This was what my daughter was like back then, day in and day out. The moment she got back from school and put down her

可沒心情聽這些，我說：「別吵！先自己去吃飯，我們正在找哥哥的學校。」

　　飯後，核算的工作終告一個段落，長久以來，因為家有考生的緊繃情緒，總算得到釋放，我在書房裡和兒子談著新學校的種種，女兒又進來了，神色詭異地說：

　　「事情爆發了！老師要你去訓導處一趟。」

　　才剛放鬆下來的心情，在聽清楚這句話後，又緊張了起來。在印象中，要求家長到訓導處，絕非好事，我差點兒從椅子上跳起來，問：

　　「什麼事爆發了？為什麼要去訓導處？」

school bag, she would follow me around the house, enumerating the day's happenings, things big and small, relevant and irrelevant. But that day, the adults were not in the mood for such small talk.

"Quiet, please! Go and eat on your own. I'm helping your brother to look for a school," I said.

We finally finished with our calculations a little bit later. Tension had been gripping the whole family for quite some time because of the all-important high school entrance exam, but at that moment, I was thankful the stress was finally relieved. However, just as my son and I started talking about the school he might be qualified for, my daughter came barging in again.

"All hell has broken loose! My teacher wants you to go see the Dean of Student Affairs," she said with an air of mystery.

An invitation to the Dean's office generally means trouble. My poor heart, which had scarcely begun to enjoy a little peace, was agitated again.

"What happened? Why the Dean's office? What for?" I almost jumped up from my chair in alarm.

女兒被我這急慌慌的表情給嚇著了，她小聲地說：

「我在學校被同學打了，那位打人的同學另外還打了別人，別人的家長告到學校去……反正，我們老師說請你到訓導處去一趟。你去了，就知道了啦！」

這下子，更讓我吃驚了！一向彬彬有禮且文弱的女兒，怎麼會捲入打架事件？又是什麼時候的事，怎麼從來沒聽她提起？我們怎麼也沒發現？

「是前一陣子，你到南京去開會的時候。有一天，我和爸爸一起在和式房間看書，爸爸看到我的腳上烏青好幾塊，問我怎麼搞的，我騙他說跌倒的，其實就是被同學打的，我怕他擔心，沒敢說。」

「同學為什麼要打你呢？你做了什麼事？」

Taken aback by my strong reaction, my daughter tried to play down the event.

"I was beaten up by a classmate. She's also beaten up other classmates. Their parents reported it to the school…. Anyway, our teacher is asking you to go to the Dean's office. Go and you'll find out."

Now, such news shocked me even more! How could my daughter, who had always been courteous and docile, get involved in a fight? When did this happen? Why did she never mention it? Why hadn't we detected anything?

"It happened quite a while ago, when you went to Nanjing for a conference. One day, when I was reading on the floor of our Japanese-style study, Dad noticed bruises on my leg and asked me about them. I lied, saying I got them in a fall. But what really happened was that I was beaten up by a classmate. I didn't tell the truth because I didn't want to worry him," she explained.

"Why did your classmate beat you up? What had you done to her?"

「我也不知道！」

　　怎麼讓人給打了，還不知道原因。事有蹊蹺，當天傍晚，我在電話中和導師溝通，更震驚地發現，毆打不止一回，女兒共被打了四次。據導師說，這是群毆事件，領導者有三位，三位都是家庭有問題的女孩子。其中一位經常扮演唆使角色的R，與外婆同住，外婆當天被請到訓導處時，還拍案怒斥訓導人員污衊她的孫女。遭受不同程度威脅或毆打的女孩有數位，其中，以我的女兒最慘，十天之內，被痛打四回，導師希望我到訓導處備案，以利訓導作業。

　　放下電話，我覺得自己的手微微發抖，我不知道，一向聒噪且和我無話不說的女兒，在我遠遊回來多日中，怎能忍住這麼殘酷悲痛的事件而不透露半點風聲。我因之確信她一定遭遇到極大的壓力，果然不

"I have no idea."

How come my daughter was beaten up and didn't even know why? Things might not be as simple as they appeared! That evening, I was in for an even greater shock when I called her teacher. My daughter was beaten up not just once, but four times! According to the teacher, the fight was initiated by three girls, all from problem families. The leader, called R, lived with her maternal grandmother. When called to the office, the grandma banged on the desk, angrily rebuking the staff for wronging her granddaughter. Quite a few girls suffered intimidation or beating of some kind, but my daughter's case was the most serious: she was beaten up four times in ten days. The teacher suggested that I formally report the case to the Dean's Office, which would facilitate an investigation.

When I put down the phone, my hands were trembling. How could my daughter, who had always been talkative and never kept anything from me, have managed to withhold from me things of such enormity, not betraying a clue of her agony all this time since I came back from Mainland China? She must have been

出所料，在外子和我款款導引下，她痛哭失聲，說：

「K威脅我，如果我敢向老師和爸媽告狀，她會從高樓上把我推下去，讓我死得很難看！」

我聽了，毛骨悚然。

女兒接著補充說：

「何況，我也怕爸、媽擔心。」

我止不住一陣心酸。平日見她溫順、講理，不容易和別人起衝突，也忽略了和她溝通類似的校園暴力的應變方法，總以為這事不會臨到她頭上，沒想到溫和的小孩，反倒成了暴力者覬覦的目標。而最讓人傷心的，莫過於沒讓小孩子對父母有足夠的信任。

tormented by the stress pent up inside of her. Just as I guessed, after a lot of prodding and coaxing by her father and me, she finally broke down. "K threatened me, saying that if I should dare to say anything to our teacher or my parents, she would push me from the top of the building, and see that I die an ugly death." she said between sobs.

I felt a chill running down my spine.

"Besides, I didn't want to worry you and Dad." she added.

I felt a stab of pain in my heart. Our daughter was a gentle and reasonable girl, who did not usually get into trouble. That's why we'd never seen the need to warn her about bullying on campus, thinking that she would never experience it. Yet, it seemed that it was her docile nature that made her an easy target for bullies and had landed her in such a plight. Even more saddening was the realization that we, as parents, had failed terribly to secure her trust in us.

　　和外子商量過後，我們決定暫緩去訓導處備案，因為，除了增加彼此的仇視外，我們不太相信，對整個事件會有任何幫助，我們決定自力救濟。當然，這其中最重要的關鍵是我們都不認為十三、四歲的孩子會真的壞到那裡去，多半是一時糊塗。尤其是知道這些孩子全是出自問題家庭，想來也是因為缺乏關愛所致，亦不免讓人思之心疼。於是，我想法子找到了主事的三位學生中的兩位T、R學生的電話號碼，K同學並非女兒的同班同學，據云居無定所，且早在警局及感化院多次出入。

　　當我在電話中客氣地說明是同學家長後，接電話的R的祖母，隨即開始破口大罵訓導人員的無的放矢，任意誣衊，足足講了數分鐘，言辭之中充滿了敵意。我靜靜聆聽了許久後，才誠懇地告訴她，我並非前來指責她的孫女，只是想了解一下狀況，祖母猶豫

After talking it over with my husband, we decided to postpone filing a formal complaint with the Dean. We believed that a formal complaint would do nothing other than worsen the situation. We decided to take the matter into our own hands. Of course, one important factor that contributed to this decision was that we did not believe that children 13 or 14 years of age were incorrigible. They were at worst misled and had temporarily gone astray. Later when I found out that all these children were from problem families, and were deprived of love and care, my heart was further softened. Consequently, I managed to find the telephone numbers of two of the three girls, T and R. The third girl K was not in my daughter's class. She reportedly had no permanent residence and had regularly been in and out of police stations and juvenile detention halls.

When I explained politely on the phone that I was a parent of a student, the grandmother of R, who answered the phone, began to berate the Dean's staff members, accusing them of groundless slander. The verbal barrage went on for quite a few minutes. I listened silently for as long as I could; then I assured her that I didn't call to condemn her granddaughter, but to get a better

了一會兒，大聲喝斥她的孫女說：

「人家的家長找到家裡來了啦！」

電話那頭傳來了模糊的聲音，似乎是女孩不肯接電話，祖母粗暴地說：

「沒關係啦！人家的媽媽很客氣的啦！」

小女孩自始至終否認曾動手打人，我原也無意強逼她認錯，只是讓她知道，家長已注意及此事，即使未親自參與毆鬥，每次都在一旁搖旗吶喊也是不該。

第二位的T在電話中振振有辭的說：

「她活該。為什麼她功課不好，我功課也不好，可是，老師每次看到她都笑瞇瞇的，看到我卻板著臉孔，我就不服氣。」

understanding of the situation. The old woman hesitated for a while; then she barked out to her granddaughter:

"Hey, her mom has come for you!"

Vague noises could be heard from the other end of the receiver, noises of resistance.

"What are you afraid of? Her mom sounded pretty polite!" the old lady blustered.

Over the phone, the young girl adamantly denied ever hitting anybody. I had no intention of forcing a confession out of her, though. My only purpose was to let her know that parents were paying attention to this matter. I reminded her that even if she didn't participate in the fighting, just egging them on was also wrong.

The second girl, T, sounded as if she had every reason for bullying my daughter.

"She deserved it! At school, I don't do well, and neither does she. But I don't understand why the teacher always greets her with a smile, and me with a long face. I can't take it!"

如此的邏輯，著實教人啼笑皆非。我委婉的開導她：

「你如果看我女兒不順眼，可以不跟她一起玩；如果我女兒有任何不對的地方，你可以直接告訴她改進，或者告訴老師或我。不管如何，動手打人都不好，阿姨聽說了女兒挨打好心疼，換做是你挨揍，你爸媽是不是也很捨不得的呀！」

T倔強地回說：

「才不哪！我爸才不會心痛，我爸說，犯錯就該被狠揍一頓。」

後來，我才知道，T在家動輒挨打，她爸打起她來，毫不留情。

當我在和兩位女孩以電話溝通時，女兒一旁緊張地屏息聆聽，不時地遞過小紙條提醒我：「拜託！不要激怒她們，要不然我會很慘。」

What ridiculous reasoning! But I needed to remain calm and patient to let her see reason. "If you don't like my daughter you don't have to be friends with her. If she does anything wrong, you can be direct and tell her; or you can tell your teacher or even tell me. No matter what, hitting people is wrong! When I heard that my daughter had been beaten up, I felt terrible! Imagine, if you were the one beaten up, wouldn't your parents feel upset?"

"No way! My dad wouldn't feel a thing! My dad says if you do wrong, you deserve a good thrashing." she answered stubbornly.

Later I found out that at home T got hit for the slightest offence. Whenever her father hit her, he spared no mercy.

Throughout the conversation, my daughter was listening nervously by my side, holding her breath. She kept passing small notes to me, reminding me: "Please, don't irritate them, of I'll have a rough time!"

我掛下電話，無言以對。

兩位女孩都接受了我的重託，答應我以後不但不再打女兒，而且還要善盡保護的責任。我相信這些半大不小的孩子是會信守承諾的，她們有她們的江湖道義，何況，確實也沒有什麼嫌隙。

事隔多日的一個中午，女兒形色倉惶的跑回家來，說是那位神龍見首不見尾的K，在逃學多日後，穿著便服在校門口出現，並揚言要再度修理女兒，幸賴T通風報信並掩護由校園後門逃出，才倖免於難。看著女兒因過度緊張而似乎縮小了一圈的臉，我不禁氣憤填膺。這是什麼世界，學校如果不能保護學生的安全，還談什麼傳道、授業、解惑！

I hung up the phone. I was speechless.

Both girls finally promised to do what I implored of them—that they would not only stop harassing my daughter, but would take it upon themselves to protect her. I believed that these "big kids" would keep their promise, in the same way men of the streets hold to their own ethical standards and sense of honor. Besides, no really big grudge existed between the kids, anyway.

However, during noon break one day, my daughter ran all the way home in a panic. She said that K, who was very elusive, suddenly showed up at the school gate after having skipped school for some time. She was not dressed in her uniform that day. She made it known that she would "fix" my daughter one more time. Fortunately, T alerted my daughter and escorted her to the backdoor, rescuing her from disaster. I looked at my daughter's face, drawn with fear, and I was filled with rage. What kind of world was this? If the school could not even ensure the safety of the students, what was the use of all those high-sounding slogans of "education," "edification," and "enlightenment"?

　　我撥電話到學校訓導處，訓導主任倒很積極，他說：「我剛才在校門口看到K，我再下去找找，找到人後，再回你電話。」

　　過了不到十分鐘，電話來了。我要求和K說話。我按捺住胸中怒火，K怯生生地叫「蔡媽媽」，我心腸立刻又軟了下來。這回，我不再問她為什麼要打人了，我慢慢了解到這些頭角崢嶸的苦悶小孩打人是不需要有什麼理由的，瞄一眼或碰一下都可以構成導火線。我問她：

　　「聽說，你一直沒到學校上課，大夥兒都到校，你一個人在外面閒逛，心裡不會慌慌的嗎？」

　　女孩兒低聲說：
　　「有時候會。」

　　「為什麼不到學校和同學一起玩、一起讀書呢？」

I phoned the Dean. He sounded very concerned and supportive. "I did have a glimpse of K at the school gate a short while ago. I'll go and find her. As soon as I get hold of her, I'll get back to you," he promised.

In less than ten minutes, the phone rang. I requested to talk to K. I had to stifle my anger before talking to her. But as soon as her timid greeting "Mama Tsai" came through the phone, my heart began to soften. This time, I did not ask her why she wanted to fight my daughter. It dawned on me that these rebellious kids needed little provocation for a fight. Things as small as a wrong look or a careless brush against them might just trigger off a fight. I tried to initiate a friendly chat with her.

"I've heard that you haven't been to school. Everybody goes to school, but you just wander about by yourself. Don't you feel bad?"

"Sometimes I do." she answered quietly.

"Why don't you go to school to be with your classmates? You can have fun and study together."

「我不喜歡上課。」

「那你喜歡什麼呢？……喜歡看小說嗎？」

「喜歡。」

我誠懇地和她說：

「阿姨家有很多散文、小說的，有空和我女兒一起來家裡玩，不要四處閒逛，有時候會碰到壞人的。」

女孩子乖乖地說了聲「謝謝！」我沉吟了一會兒，終究沒提打人的事。嘆了口氣，掛了電話，眼淚流了一臉。是什麼樣的環境把孩子逼得四處為家？是什麼樣的父母，忍心讓孩子流落街頭？我回頭遵照訓導主任的指示，叮嚀女兒：

「以後再有類似狀況，就跑到訓導處去，知道嗎？」

"But I don't like going to class." she said.

"Then what do you like? Do you like reading novels?"

"I guess so."

I wanted her to feel my sincerity for her. "There're a lot of books in my house…novels, stories. When you're free, come to our house with my daughter. Don't wander the streets. You may run into bad people."

The girl politely said thank you. Meanwhile I was struggling inside whether to mention the fights, but finally decided against it. I hung up the phone with a sigh, and my face was covered with tears. What kind of environment had made this child "homeless," I wondered. What kind of parents would let their child wander the streets? As for my daughter, I followed the Dean's suggestions and told her:

"Next time when something like this happens again, go and get help from the Dean's office. Do you understand?" I said emphatically.

女兒委屈地說：

「你以為我不想這樣做嗎？他們圍堵我，我根本去不了。」

過了幾天，兒子從母校的操場打球回來，邊擦汗邊告訴我：「今天在學校打球時，身後有人高喊K的名字，我回頭看，遜斃了！又瘦又小，妹妹太沒用了，是我就跟她拚了。」

女兒不服氣地反駁說：

「你別看她瘦小，那雙眼睛瞪起人來，教人不寒而慄，好像要把人吃掉一樣，嚇死人哪！」

事情總算解決了，因為據女兒說，從那以後，再沒人找過她麻煩，我們都鬆了口氣，慶幸漫天陰霾全開。

"Do you think I didn't want to do that? When they surrounded me I simply couldn't go anywhere," my daughter sounded as if she had been terribly wronged.

A few days later, my son came back from playing basketball at his old school, and told us what had happened that day. "While I was playing ball today, somebody shouted out K's name. I turned my head and I saw her. What a pipsqueak! Sister is a real wimp to be afraid of her! I'd have fought it out with her," he said, wiping away his sweat.

My daughter raised her objections immediately. "You don't know her like I do! She's thin and small alright, but sometimes her mad dog eyes send shivers down your spine. You feel as if she is going to pounce upon you and tear you to pieces! It's scary!"

But in the ensuing days, there seemed to be peace. According to my daughter, nobody had given her any more trouble. We were relieved and thankful that the whole thing seemed to have blown over.

今年年初，《中國時報》舉辦兩岸三邊華文小說研討會，一連兩天，我在誠品藝文空間參與盛會。那夜，回到家，外子面露憂色說：「很奇怪哦！女兒這個星期假日，成天埋首寫東西，畫著細細的格子，密密麻麻的，不知寫些什麼，不讓我看。」

夜深了，孩子快上床，我進到女兒房裡和她溝通，我問她是不是有什麼事要和我說，她起先說沒有，我說：

「我們不是說好了，我們之間沒有祕密嗎？」

女兒從書包裡掏出那些紙張，大約有五、六張之多，前後兩面都寫得滿滿的，全是她做的噩夢和那回被打的經過，像是在警察局錄口供似的，我看了不禁淚如雨下，差點兒崩潰。原先以為不過是小孩之間的

Early this year I attended a cross-straits conference on Chinese fiction sponsored by the *China Times.* For two full days I participated in that literary gathering at Eslite Art Gallery. Then, when I came back home that evening, my husband confided to me something that had obviously upset him.

"Something strange is going on! For the whole weekend, our daughter just buried herself in writing. She drew lines on the paper and filled them up with her small handwriting. I have no clue what she was writing about. She wouldn't let me have a look."

That night, as the children were finally ready for bed, I went into my daughter's room to be alone with her. I asked her whether she had something to tell me. She said no, but I wouldn't settle for that. "Haven't we made deal? We've promised each other that there would be no secrets between us." I reminded her.

She took out pages of writing from her school bag. There were about five or six of them, written on both sides. They were vivid descriptions of her nightmares and details about her being beaten up, very much like the transcription of a police interrogation. As I read them, tears came pouring out like rain. I almost broke down.

情緒性發洩，沒想到是如此血淋淋的校園暴力。

　　女兒細細的小字寫著：

　　第一次：那一天是星期五，十五班的K跑來，叫我放學後在校門口等她。下課後，她打扮得花枝招展在門口等我，還噴了香水。她把我騙到隔壁XX國宅二樓，我才放下書包，一轉身，她就變了一個臉，凶狠地問我一個我聽不懂的問題，我還來不及回答，她就打了我好幾個耳光，我愣了一下，她打我？我真是不敢相信？我和她無怨無仇，她為什麼打我？我跟她扭打在一起，她拉我的頭髮，我扯她衣服，她抓住我的頭髮把我丟出去，我整個跪到地下，也就是所謂的『一敗塗地』，她把我從地上拉起來恐嚇我『你要是敢講出來，我就把你從樓上推下去』，我怕得要命，因為氣喘病發，正喘著氣，突然從圍觀的人群中跑出來一個年約二十左右的女人對我吼：『你還喘！喘死

At first I thought it was just a child's way of venting her anger, but it turned out to be a true story of grim and gory campus violence.

In her small handwriting, she gave the following account:

The first time: It was a Friday. K of Class 15 came and told me to see her at the school gate after school. When school was over, there she was, dressed attractively, even wearing perfume. She lured me to the apartment building next door. We went to the second floor. I had only just put down my school bag and turned round when she barked out a question totally incomprehensible to me, her countenance a total turnaround from a moment ago. Before I had time to answer, she slapped my face a few times. I was in a daze. She slapped me! I couldn't believe it! I'd never done anything to her, and there had never been any reason for a grudge. Why would she hit me? I hit back. Then the two of us got into a fight, with her pulling my hair and me tugging at her clothes. She grabbed me by the hair, trying to fling me down but ended up bringing me to my knees, so that I was "totally defeated," so to speak. But that's not all. The next moment, she grabbed me from the floor, growling a threat: "If you dare to tell anyone about this, I'll push you off from here!" I was scared to death. The whole thing got my asthma going, and as I was gasping for breath, a twenty-something-

啊！』說完，又給我一個耳光，我整個人又跪到地上去。我因為害怕，什麼都聽她的，出了國宅，我真的忍不住哭了！我哭的原因是因為我好膽小，而且我不甘心啊！我竟然就這樣傻傻地被她打！她還說我說話很ㄅㄧㄠ∨，ㄅㄧㄠ∨是什麼意思啊？我從來沒有這樣屈辱過，連爸媽都從來沒有打過我啊！她憑什麼打我？我恨死她了，我生平沒恨過什麼人，我發誓與她勢不兩立。

第二次：暑期輔導中午，K突然從校外跑來（她沒有參加輔導），約我去國宅十二樓talk talk，我很膽小，不敢反抗，只好乖乖地跟她去，一到十二樓，她就說：『上次你扯我衣服，害我整個曝光，你今天是要裸奔回去？還是被我打？』她看起來很生氣的樣子，我考慮了一下，就選擇挨打，她打人很奇特，

year-old woman suddenly came out of the small crowd of bystanders, yelling at me: "Wheeze till you drop, sweetheart!" To that, she added another slap on my face. I was brought down to my knees again. I was so scared that I had to obey everything she said. When I left that apartment building, I burst out crying. I cried because I hated myself for being such a wimp. Besides, I couldn't swallow such humiliation! I couldn't accept the fact that I had been roughed up like this, without the slightest knowledge of why. She said I talked in a "cocky" way, what does "cocky" mean? I have never been so humiliated! I've never been hit by anybody, not even by my parents! What right did she have to hit me? I hate her! I've never hated anybody in my life, but now I've decided that we're sworn enemies!"

The second time: At noon one day during summer school, K, who didn't attend summer school, suddenly appeared. She asked me to have a talk on the twelfth floor of the apartment building where she had fought me last time. Since I didn't have the guts to say no, I followed her obediently. As soon as we arrived, she said: "Last time, you pulled my clothes, almost stripping me naked. Today, you have a choice: run home naked, or get slugged." She looked scary. After a moment's thinking, I chose the latter. She had a peculiar way of hitting people.

不只是打臉，連後腦勺一起打，我被她打得臉熱辣辣的，腫得像豬頭皮似的，我實在痛得受不了了，請她等一下。我用手往牙齒一摸，手上都是血！她凶狠地說：『今天饒了你，算你走狗運！』走的時候，又恐嚇我不准講，要不然會死得很難看……

第三次：這一次本來是要找班上另一位同學的麻煩的，那位同學跑了，所以就找我，她們又問我一些莫名其妙的問題，問一句，揍我一下，這一次真的很慘，T、K二人連打帶踢地弄得我全身是傷，膝蓋上一大塊青腳印，久久不消，這次，嘴巴又流了好多血，啊！我真是沒用啊……

第四次：這次是在參觀資訊大樓時，T把我堵到廁所裡，又是拳打腳踢……

K，我到底是哪裡讓你看不順眼，為什麼一定要

She hit not only my face but also the back of my head. My face felt burning hot, and my head seemed to have swollen to the size of a basketball. The pain was so excruciating that I begged her to stop. I touched my teeth and there was blood on my hand. "I'm letting you off today and you're damn lucky I do!" While I was leaving, she threatened me again: "one word of this and you will die...."

The third time: This time, they had planned to "fix" another classmate, but she escaped, and I became the substitute. Again they asked a few off-the-wall questions; each question was accompanied by a punch. It was pretty rough. With T and K hitting and kicking me together, I was hurt all over. There was a dark bruise on my knee, which took a long time to heal. Like last time, my mouth bled badly. On, I'm such a coward!..."

"The fourth time: While the class was visiting the Technology and Information Center, T pushed me into the rest room, hit and kicked me....

"K, have I done anything so wrong that I'm such a nuisance to you?

動手打人呢？這樣你又有什麼好呢！這樣打人是要
被⋯⋯

　　有一天我夢到我當上了警察，我們組長要我去
XX國宅抓兩名通緝犯，一是Ｋ，一是Ｔ，我到XX國
宅時，果然看到她們又在打人，我立刻上前制止，趁
機從背後將Ｋ的雙手反扣，交給同事帶回局裡；再轉
身冷冷地朝Ｔ說：『我這一次放你走，希望你改過，
別讓我再抓到，不要讓我失望。』她問我：『你到底
是誰？』我把證件拿給她看，她嚇了一跳，馬上向我
下跪。⋯⋯

　　前兩天我又夢到Ｋ，她完全失去了凶狠的眼神，
變得脆弱不堪，我勸她：『回家去吧！再不回家，你
媽要得相思病了！』Ｋ問我是誰？我告訴她，我就是
以前被她打三次的人，我勸她改過向善，並幫她找回

Why do you have to beat up people? What good does it do you? It only makes you....

"One day I dreamed that I'd become a police officer. Our section chief wanted me to go to some apartment building to catch two criminals who were on the run—and they were K and T. When I got there, I could see that they were beating up people. I went up immediately to stop them. Then I grabbed K's arms, handcuffed her from behind and handed her over to my colleague to be taken back to the police station. Then I turned to talk to T, rather coldly. 'This time, I'm letting you off. I'm giving you a chance to change your ways. Don't let me catch you again. Don't let me down.' 'Who the heck are you?' asked T. I showed her my ID. She was so scared that she immediately knelt down in front of me....."

"The other day, I dreamed of K again. Her eyes had completely lost their hard look. She looked forlorn. 'Go home! If you don't go home, your mother will be worried sick.' I tried to persuade her. K asked me who I was. I told her I was the person she'd beaten up three times. I persuaded her to change her ways and be good. I even helped her to find

了媽媽，她高興地流下了眼淚⋯⋯

⋯⋯⋯⋯⋯

　　我一邊看，一邊流淚，這才知道，我們的一念之仁是如何虧待了善良的女兒，那樣的暴行對她造成的傷害遠遠超過我們的想像，而那些施暴的孩子的行徑，著實可用「可恨」或「可惡」來形容，我必須慚愧的承認，如果我早知道那些孩子是如此殘忍地對待我的女兒！我是絕不會那樣委曲求全地去和行凶者打交道的，我也深信，沒有任何一個母親會加以容忍的，我是多麼對不起女兒呀！

　　可是，事隔半年，為什麼會突然又舊事重提呢？

　　「不是答應過媽媽，把這件事徹底忘掉嗎？」

her mother. She was so happy that she shed tears of joy...

....

As I was reading, I couldn't fight back my tears. Only then did I realize that we had shown sentimental kindness to evil only at the expense of our daughter. Such acts of cruelty as she had suffered had done far greater damage to her than we had imagined. Such behavior was really detestable, abominable! I had to admit with shame that if I had known what atrocities those kids were capable of inflicting upon my daughter, I'd have not been so merciful when I dealt with those two little brutes. I earnestly believe that no mother in the world would ever tolerate such cruelty to her children. How shameful that I have failed in my responsibility to protect my daughter!

But all these things had happened about half a year ago. I wondered why they had come back to haunt her again.

"Didn't you promise Mom that you would forget the whole thing and let bygones be bygones?" I asked my daughter.

　　「最近考試，老師重新排位置，那兩位曾經打我的T、R同學，一位坐我左邊，一位坐我前面，我覺得好害怕！雖然她們已經不再打我了，可是，我想到以前的事，就忍不住發抖。……」

　　我摟著女兒，心裡好痛好痛，我安慰她：
　　「讓我去和老師商量，請老師掉換一下位置好嗎？」

　　女兒全身肌肉緊縮，緊張地說：
　　「不要！到時候她們萬一知道了，我又倒楣了。我答應你不再害怕就是了！」

　　外子和我徹夜未眠，不知如何是好，女兒柔弱，無法保護自己，強硬的手段，恐怕只會給她帶來更大的傷害，我們第一次認真地考慮到轉學問題。一連幾天，我打電話問了幾間私立教會學校，全說轉學得經

"Recently, because of the exam, the teacher rearranged the seats. T and R, who used to bully me, are now seated to my left and to my front. I'm scared! Though they no longer bully me, I can't help trembling whenever I think of what happened in the past...."

I hugged my daughter. My heart was greatly troubled. "Let me talk to the teacher. Let me ask her to rearrange the seating. How about that?" I tried to comfort her.

At that, my daughter's whole body tensed up. She was all nerves. "No, if they find out about it, I'll be in for it! I promise I'll stand up to them!" she pleaded.

My husband and I could not sleep all night. We were at the end of our rope. Our daughter was meek, totally defenseless. We had to deal with the situation carefully, or she would be traumatized even more. For the first time, we mulled over the possibility of transferring her to another school. For the next few

過學科考試，篩選十分嚴格。想到女兒不甚理想的學科成績，只好快快然打退堂鼓，上帝原來也要揀選智慧高的子民，全不理會柔弱善良的百姓。我在從學校回家的高速公路上，望著前面筆直坦蕩的公路，覺得前途茫茫，一時之間，悲不自勝，竟至涕泗滂沱。

正當我們幾乎是心力交瘁時，女兒回來高興地報告：

「老師說，下禮拜又要重新排位置。媽媽不要再擔心了。……媽媽，真是對不起。」

那夜，我終於背著女兒和導師聯絡，請她在重換位置時，注意一下，是不是能儘量避免讓他們坐在一塊兒。老師知道情況後連連抱歉，並答應儘快改進，臨掛電話前，導師說：

days, we called a few private Christian schools, but their answer was the same—transfer students had to take a series of stringent screening tests. When I thought of my daughter's lackluster academic performance, I sadly abandoned this idea. Inside I was even grumbling that God seemed to favor intelligent people more than weak ones. Driving home from school, staring at the bleak highway in front of me, I felt that our future was equally bleak. At that moment, I was overcome with grief. And in the loneliness of my car, I cried.

Just when we were physically and emotionally almost completely drained, our daughter came back one day with some good news.

"The teacher said that she would rearrange our seats next week. Nothing to worry about any more!…Mama, I'm really sorry."

This had finally come as a result of my conversation with her teacher. One night I finally decided to talk to the teacher without my daughter's knowledge. I suggested that my daughter should be seated away from those two girls when the time came to rearrange the seats. When the teacher knew what my daughter had been

「你那女兒實在可愛，她一點也不記仇，上次班際拔河比賽，她拚命為T加油，我一旁看著她喉嚨都喊啞了，臉紅嘟嘟的……我有時候上了一天課，好辛苦，偶爾上課時，朝她的方向望過去，她總不忘給我一個甜甜的笑容，蔡太太，你也是當老師的，應該會知道，那種窩心的感覺，當老師的快樂不就是這樣嗎？真是讓人心疼的孩子！」

第二天傍晚，孩子放學回來，我聽從導師的建議，和女兒一起到七樓陽臺上把她寫的那些密密麻麻的紙條全燒光，希望這些不愉快的記憶隨著燒光的紙片兒灰飛煙滅。

紙片兒終於燒成灰燼！我轉過身拿掃把想清掃灰燼時，突然一陣風吹過來，把紙灰一股腦全吹上了天

through, she apologized profusely and promised to remedy the situation as soon as possible. Before hanging up the phone, she shared with me her favorable impressions of my daughter.

"That daughter of yours is really adorable! Despite everything, she bears no grudge against any of the girls. During the last tug-of-war competition between the classes, she cheered T on. I noticed that she almost shouted herself hoarse, and her chubby face was very pink. For me, sometimes a whole day's teaching can be draining, but during class, when I catch her eye, she will always give me a smile. Mrs. Tsai, you're also a teacher. You should understand the kind of feeling that makes a teacher's hard work worthwhile. Your daughter is really a lovely child!"

Toward evening the next day when my daughter came back from school, I followed the teacher's advice and went with her to the roof on the seventh floor. We set all her writings on fire. We hoped that the devastating memories could be consigned to the past.

The pages were finally reduced to ashes. When I turned round for a broom to clean them up, a gust of wind had already blown

空，女兒惘然望著蒼天，幽幽地說：

「如果記憶像風就好了。」

記憶真的會像風嗎？

——原載一九九四年五月二日《中國時報》

收入九歌新版《如果記憶像風》（2011年）

them away. My daughter stared into the sky, as if in a trance. "If only memories were like the wind," she said quietly to herself.

Will our memories really be like the wind?

"The Chinese PEN" **Autumn, 2005**

我為卿狂
Crazy About You

胡守芳／譯

Translated by Shou-Fang HU-MOORE

　　幾個月來，我不知和那株芒果樹照面幾十次，卻從不曾看見芒果樹下的路面上有任何一顆掉落的芒果，連被車子輾過的屍首也無，這群芒果們很堅持地盤據枝頭，好像正玩著誰先落下誰就輸了的遊戲。雖然無法計算芒果的多寡，但只要一抬頭，就一定讓人眼花撩亂、引得人忽忽若狂，芒果似乎從春末到仲夏，一個不能少地彼此約定著。

無意間發現，那般纍纍的土芒果，就懸掛在巷道的半空中，讓人垂涎欲滴。

從四月起，每次回老家，開車時，我總刻意繞道，不斷地跟它行注目禮。那棵芒果樹還真偉壯，開枝散葉，幾乎將整個天空遮蔽。車子行經其下，低枝下的芒果，差不多就垂到車頂上方約一、兩公尺處，探身出去，只要稍稍「喬」一下身體的姿勢，舉起手就能一把抓上幾十個，可惜總不能，因為外子就像便衣警察隨侍在側，口頭警告之不足，往往還加快車速前進，絕不讓我有可乘之機，而唯恐我無端鬧出亂子，這位可恨的警察還緊迫盯人地如影隨形，每次不斷進行精神訓話，從「禮義廉恥，國之四維」開始，直複習到民法不知道第幾章為止。我屢次擺脫監視不果，氣得差一點跟他鬧離婚。

It was an unexpected discovery. Hanging right in midair above the alley, clusters upon clusters of Taiwan *Soai-a* mango looked so delicious they made my mouth water.

Since April this year, each time while driving back to my old hometown, I made a detour over there on purpose to take a look. The mango tree was so huge that its branches and leaves almost blocked the entire sky. As we drove past it, the mangos hanging on the lower branches were only a couple of meters from the top of our car. Had I but "repositioned" myself slightly and extened my arm, dozens of them would have fallen into my hands. But unfortunately I had not been able to do so, because my husband was always by my side watching like a plain-clothes cop. Besides verbally warning me off the attempt, he often sped past it to avoid giving me any opportunity. For fear that I should try to make trouble, this detestable cop even followed me around like a shadow, constantly lecturing me about the ethics of being an upstanding citizen and quoting from civil law regarding penalties for theft. After many attempts to shake him off, yet to no avail, I became so frustrated I almost wanted to divorce him.

芒果長成那般張狂真是不應該！從綠轉紅再翻黃，幾個月裡，它夙夜匪懈地在顏色及體積上推陳出新。越來越大的芒果，在我胸腔發酵、膨脹，我感覺幾乎要爆炸了！芒果樹就直挺挺地矗立在隔壁巷子的某一家空屋的院子內，大門深鎖，夜裡屋內黑漆漆的，顯見主人早已棄守、搬離，徒然留下一樹招搖的芒果。巧的是左右相鄰的屋子，也是一樣人去樓空，連打探主人消息都不可得。以此之故，芒果雖然結實纍纍，卻無人聞問。

屬於我的這場芒果熱，足足維持了三個多月，從開花到青綠的小芒果到黃橙的熟芒果，我日思夜夢，外子怎麼也想不通其中的道理。不過就幾個芒果嘛！他老是這麼勸慰我：

「你喜歡吃芒果，看要幾個，我如數奉贈！菜市

How could those mangos grow so shamelessly wild! Changing from green to red and then yellow, they underwent continuous transformations both in color and size within a few months. As the mangos became bigger and bigger, something in my chest also began to ferment and swell, bringing me to the brink of explosion. The mango tree stood straight and tall in the yard of an empty house in the alley next to ours. With the gate tightly locked and the whole building pitch dark in the night, the house had obviously been abandoned by the owner, leaving behind all the mangos swaying in midair. The odd thing was that the houses on both sides were not occupied either, making it impossible for me to find out the whereabouts of the owner. As a result, although the tree was laden so thick with mangos, no one had been picking them.

My mango fever lasted more than three months. I dreamt about them day and night, from the time they first bloomed and through the green stage until they were fully ripe. My husband couldn't understand why. To him, they were just some mangos. He often tried to console me with these words, "If you like mangos, I'll buy you as many as you want. There are lots of them in the market. With a high yield this year, they are inexpensive and sweet-tasting.

場裡多的是！今年芒果大出，又便宜又好吃！愛吃幾個買幾個，你幹麼那麼想不開！」

他還是不懂！不是買不買的問題！我就是見不得它高掛天際，沒人打理、無人關心！

我對芒果一向有近乎病態的迷戀，迷戀的原因，可追溯到幼年時後窗望出去的那株屬於四伯家的芒果樹。一到了四、五月，也同樣結實纍纍，母親總耳提面命：

「絕不能去偷採，別人家的東西，誰要不聽話，小心皮癢！」

什麼「別人家的東西」！明明就是四伯家的。偏偏越是被明令禁止的事，越是讓人亢奮難擋，這是孩童叛逆的鐵律。四合院裡大家庭難解的糾葛，常常一觸即發，而導火線往往從細事發端，母親想是為了防

Buy as many as you want. Why are you so obsessed with it?"

He simply doesn't get it. It is not a matter of buying or not. I just cannot leave them hanging there in midair with no one to attend to and care for them.

I have always had a near-morbid infatuation with mango. The cause of this infatuation may be traced back to the mango tree in my Fourth Uncle's yard, which was visible from the back window of our home when I was a child. Each year when April and May came about, it would also be laden with fruit. My mother dinned warnings into our ears all the time, "Don't ever steal. They are other people's property. Whoever disobeys will get smacked!"

What did she mean by "other people's property"? The Fourth Uncle is not OTHER PEOPLE! The more one is admonished against doing something, the more irresistible it becomes. It is a cast-iron law governing children's rebellion. With an extended family living in a quadrangle, inextricable disputes among family

範未然，卻不知那樣斬釘截鐵的罰則在孩童的心裡引發多大的波瀾！看得到卻吃不著真是折騰人，過度壓抑的結果，導致我一生都虎虎地注視著，彷彿永遠都沒有饜足的時刻，看到芒果，直覺就是撲過去，義無反顧！六歲以前的記憶幾乎被歲月沖刷得七零八落，只有窗後的那棵芒果樹，彷彿踩著流轉的光陰日漸茁壯，不是駐足在菜市場裡、超市中，就是停留在親朋家的果盤內，甚至陌生的人家圍牆邊，尤其是掛在枝頭上的，特別引人亢奮。

也許這樣的理由還不足以道盡芒果熱的緣由，某些性格的人似乎就是容易為「數大即是美」所惑。回想三十餘年前第一次到外子家面見未來的公婆，一踏進他們家的四合院，即刻被一株長滿果實的芭樂樹迷

members can often be triggered at any moment. And the fuse more often than not is but a small incident. My mother was simply trying to nip it in the bud. However, she didn't realize how much disturbance such a resolute decree created in a child's mind. It was really tormenting to look at something and not be able to eat it. This over-suppression made me eye the mango like a prey throughout my life. There seemed to be never a satiated moment for me. I felt an urge to pounce on it at sight without any hesitation. Nearly all of my memories before age six have been washed away by time, except for that mango tree outside the window. It appears to grow stronger and stronger with the passing of time. The fruit show up in the markets, on the fruit plate in the home of relatives and friends, and even beside the fence of strangers' houses. Particularly the ones hanging on the branches get me excited the most.

Perhaps this reasoning is not sufficient to explain the cause of my mango-fever. People with a certain type in personality seem prone to be attracted by the "beauty of masses". I recall the first time I went to visit my future parents-in-law at their home thirty-some years ago. On setting foot in the courtyard of their

得神魂顛倒。還沒走入大廳，先就執起一旁閒置（用
「待命」二字可能更恰切些）的帶網竹竿，興奮且盡
情地狂掃、猛摘，心裡充滿了前所未有的滿足感。其
後，嫂嫂、姊姊們奉命到男方家看門風，也無法克制
地臣服在那棵芭樂樹下。就這樣，為了一棵芭樂樹，
全家毫無異議地決定讓我賠上終身。可見，纍纍的果
實魅力不可小覷！

　　那位嚴守紀律的便衣警察，當年看見我為高掛的
芭樂癡狂，他的反應跟現在可謂大不相同，見證了男
人婚前、婚後判若兩人。當年他認為我「天真浪漫，
痴得可愛」；現在卻說「莫名其妙，不顧形象」！
不知是進入婚姻後便浪漫盡失，抑或歲月真的催人現
實。

quadrangle I was captivated by a guava tree laden with fruit. I didn't wait to enter the lobby before picking up a bamboo pole with a net, which was "laying idle" on the side (or perhaps more appropriately "standing by"), and going on a harvesting frenzy. While doing this, I was overwhelmed with a sense of satisfaction that I had never experienced before. Later on, as my older sisters and sisters-in-law were sent over to check up on the family of my future husband, they couldn't resist the charm of that guava tree either. Thus, for the sake of a guava tree, I was given away in marriage without any objection from my own family. It just shows that one cannot underestimate the power of a tree laden with fruit.

In comparison with what happens now, the reaction of that plain-clothes cop at the time was certainly quite different when he saw my infatuation for the guavas hanging on the tree. It proves that men behave differently before and after marriage. In those days he thought that I looked "innocent, romantic and delightfully infatuated", but today his comment about me has become "baffling behaviour and disregard of self-image". I don't know whether it is because he has lost all the romantic feelings after being married or because life can actually turn one into a pragmatist.

　　跟我媽一樣，他老為了我覬覦別人的芒果而忐忑
不安。剛開始，我也不過隨口說說，並不十分當真：

　　「哇！趕快停下車來，我們想辦法摘一個吧！太
過分了！長那麼多。」

　　沒料到他竟正經八百地拿我當孩子訓話：
　　「你怎麼會這樣！別人家的芒果欸！虧你還是教
授！」

　　「教授是怎樣！法律上不是規定長到別人家院子
的水果，那家人可以合法就地採摘！」我立刻以自身
都不知是否正確的法律知識唬弄他。

　　「可是，這些芒果又沒長到我們家的院子裡
來！」

　　「它是沒長到我們家的院子，它若是長到我們的

Like my mother, he always feels uneasy about my coveting the mangos in other people's yards. At the very beginning I was only making casual remarks without real intention, such as "Wow, stop the car right now. Let's find a way to pick one. It's too unbearable to see so much fruit up there!"

Little did I know that he would take it so seriously and lecture me as if I were a child, "What's wrong with you? Those mangos belong to others. You ought to know better, for a professor!"

"So what if I am a professor? According to the law, isn't it legal to pick the fruit off one's neighbour's tree if the branches carrying the fruit extend into one's yard?" I immediately tried to bluff him with my smattering of legal knowledge which I wasn't even sure to be true or not.

"But, those mangos are not in our yard!"

"It's true that they are not in our yard. It would have been

院子來，如今就不必如此大費周章囉！⋯⋯可是，它長到圍牆外的巷道來，巷道是公有地，所謂『公有』，就是屬於大夥兒所有，不是人人得而採之嗎？⋯⋯而且，你不覺得這家人很可惡嗎？任憑這些芒果囂張地怒長著，也不處理，引誘別人犯罪嘛！」

這位便衣警察一向口拙，從來沒有在辯論中占過上風，這回也不例外。但微笑不語並不代表心悅誠服，他的專長是沉默地堅持重整道德的意志力。我們結婚數十年，他一直力圖對抗我隨時萌生的「詭異想法」和劍及履及的實踐精神。

其實，原先我也是一名他口中的良民，曾經趁他不留神的午後，去按那個廢宅子的門鈴，想依循正常管道澆熄心頭的熱火。但是，既然經長期觀察後被判定是廢宅，自然是沒有人前來應門。我訕訕然站在門

much easier IF they were actually in our yard! … However, they have overgrown to the alley. An alley is a 'public space'. Being 'public' means that they belong to us all. Anyone can pick them, right? … Besides, don't you think that the people living in that house are quite disgusting? They simply let the mangos overgrow without doing anything about it. They blatantly tempt people to commit theft!"

Being slow with words, the plain-clothes cop had never won any debate before and it was no exception this time. But his quiet smile didn't mean that he was convinced. His strength lies in his will power to insist on restoring morals in a quiet manner. After being married for several decades, he has always tried very hard to confront my impulsive "bizarre ideas" and my vigour to put them into practice right away.

But in fact, I had initially been one of his so-called 'good citizens'. One afternoon I went behind his back to the abandoned house to ring the door bell, intending to pursue the normal channel and quench the fire of impulse in me. Yet, since my long-time observation had determined the house to be vacant, there

口，仰頭看到那一樹茂密到無法收拾的芒果——少說幾百顆，忽然眼淚不自禁地流了下來——不過想摘個芒果而已！竟然如此困難重重。而可以想見的是，這些無人打理、自生自滅的芒果，將寂然地自行委地，就不說有多暴殄天物，也枉費它三、四個月來的花枝招展。

六月底，我實在受不了煎熬，有一度還心生歹念，慫恿外子幫忙一起搬運扶梯，趁月黑風高之際，前去一解相思。我知道外子一向奉公守法，絕不容許我胡來，所以，極力保證：

「就去摸一下就好！絕不摘！哎呀！就摸一下，過過乾癮也好。夫妻一場，你就成全、成全我吧！」

外子聽我這麼說，簡直驚訝到極點，立刻以我所熟知的典故回應：

was naturally no one answering the door. I stood ill at ease in front of the door and saw at least several hundreds of mangos hanging closely together above me. Tears suddenly rolled down my cheeks uncontrollably. All I wanted was to pick ONE, yet it was so difficult. It's only to be expected that these mangos that had been left to grow on their own would fall to the ground to rot alone. Several months of luxuriant growth would be all in vain, not to mention the reckless waste of Nature's product.

At the end of June, I finally reached the limits of my endurance. Once I even thought to solicit help from my husband to carry a ladder to the site in the middle of the night in order to quench my longing. I knew my husband had always been a law-abiding citizen and wouldn't allow me to do anything wrong. Therefore, I promised fervently, "I'll only touch them for a moment. I WON'T pick at all! Ai-yah, just one touch to satisfy my craving! We've been husband and wife all these years. Please grant my wish just this once."

My husband was extremely shocked to hear this. He immediately responded by quoting a literary allusion I was familiar

「虧你還是中國文學博士！古人不是曾經說過：
『君子防未然，不處嫌疑間。瓜田不納履，李下不整
冠。』」你還想公然搬梯子去芒果樹下，誰信你只是
去摸一下，沒有竊盜的居心！……要去你自己去，我
才不當幫凶。怎麼會有你這樣奇怪的人！」

人家說：「夫妻同心，其利斷金」，遇到這樣不
解風情的丈夫，我只能徒呼奈何。何況，他還引經據
典的，看起來國學常識還滿豐富的！

七月中旬，芒果已肥碩到不可思議的地步，再不
採摘，眼見一顆顆就要陣亡。隔著一個巷子，我在
屋裡走來踱去，就不知這場熱鬧該如何收拾？外子聽
說我為芒果的結局焦躁不安，好像想起什麼似地朝我
說：

with, "How could you be a PhD in Chinese Literature? Didn't the ancients say, 'A man of moral integrity takes preventive measures to avoid being in a situation that may arouse suspicion. Don't pull on your shoes in a melon patch, nor adjust your cap under a plum tree.' You are now even thinking to carry a ladder to the mango tree out in the open. Who will believe that you only want to touch and have no intention to steal them? ... If you want to go, go by yourself. I won't be your accomplice. What a strange person you are!"

There has been a saying: "Husband and wife of the same mind are like a sharp blade that can cut through metal." Yet, having a husband who is too thick to read my mind, I could only bemoan my fate. What's more, since he even quoted the classics, it looked like he knew quite a bit about Chinese classics.

By mid-July, those mangos had become very large and fleshy. If there was still no one to pick them, they would all soon "bite the dust". Here I was pacing back and forth in my house just a lane away, not knowing how the drama would end. After learning about my anxiety towards the fate of the mangos, my husband seemed to recall something and said to me, "Oh, by the way, this morning

　　「對了！今早，錯過了垃圾車，我直追到後面的巷子，忽然看到芒果樹的那家門戶洞開，連院子內的中門都開著，本來想進去跟他們打打招呼，順便替你問候一下他們家的芒果。沒想到，倒了垃圾回頭，裡頭的門卻又關了。我站在那裡想了想，覺得為了芒果打招呼有些滑稽，就算了！」

　　「什麼！就這樣算了！你明明知道太太這樣朝思暮想，你就這樣算了！好不容易有人在裡面，你就不能為我……要是你不敢，為什麼回來不趕緊告訴我，讓我自己去交涉？」

　　我想，外子一定挺後悔不小心說溜了嘴，他懊惱地說：
　　「回到家就忘了啊！又不是什麼重要的事！」

　　我顧不得跟他抬槓，立刻衝出冷氣室！往後巷奔

I missed the garbage truck and ran after it to the alley behind us. I happened to notice the gate of the house with the mango tree wide open. The entrance door facing the front yard was also open. Initially I was going to walk over to say hello, and to inquire about the mangos for you as well. Yet, by the time I got back there after dumping the garbage,the door had already been closed. I stood there and thought for a moment. It felt somewhat funny to say hello for the sake of some mangos, so I decided to forget about it."

"What! That's it? You know all too well that your wife has been yearning for them day and night. Yet you just forgot about it. Finally there was someone there, why couldn't you do the asking for me? … If you didn't have the guts, why didn't you tell me on getting home and let me deal with it?"

I think my husband truly regretted that he lost his tongue accidentally. Feeling annoyed, he said, "I forgot to mention it after coming back. After all, it's not something too important!"

I couldn't be bothered to argue with him and immediately

去。芒果樹依然紋風不動地豎立，芒果依然垂實纍
纍，露出撩人的姿態。大門深鎖，我急驚風似地按了
門鈴，沒人應；再按，還是沒人；再按，回應我的，
依舊是沉默。我越按越傷心，不知怎地竟絕望得想嚎
啕大哭。回頭走，邊掉淚，邊暗自發誓，絕不再為這
群芒果瞎操心：

「管他的！隨便它愛怎樣就怎樣！反正，浪費是
那家人的事，掉到地上爛掉也不干我的事，雷公也不
會打我。」

放下心思以後，彷彿海闊天空起來。

我開始理性地思考其中的若干啟人疑竇之處。譬
如：幾個月來，我不知和那株芒果樹照面幾十次，
卻從不曾看見芒果樹下的路面上有任何一顆掉落的芒
果，連被車子輾過的屍首也無，這群芒果們很堅持地
盤據枝頭，好像正玩著誰先落下誰就輸了的遊戲。雖

ran out of the air-conditioned room, dashing towards the lane behind us. The mango tree stood absolutely still and the clusters of fruit were hanging there in the usual attractive manner. The gate of the house was bolted. I rang the door bell as if there were an emergency, but no one answered. I pressed it again and again, but there was still only silence. The more I rang the bell the more heartbroken I became. I felt so desperate that I nearly burst out crying. As my tears kept falling on my way home, I secretly swore that I would never worry about those mangos again: "Who cares! Let it be! That's their waste after all. It's none of my business if they fall onto the ground and rot. The Thunder God won't punish me for it."

After letting go of my obsession, my mind seemed to open up.

I began to comb through some suspicious points rationally. For instance, I lost account of how many times I had seen that mango tree during those few months, but never for once did I see a mango on the ground beneath the tree. There wasn't any evidence of them being run over by the cars either. Those mangos insisted on holding onto the branches, as if they were playing a

然無法計算芒果的多寡，但只要一抬頭，就一定讓人眼花撩亂、引得人忽忽若狂，芒果似乎從春末到仲夏，一個不能少地彼此約定著。而路過的行人及附近的鄰居不在少數，何以芒果們竟能安然無恙地存活？有人說：

「用膝蓋想也知道，小學課本裡早說過了！芒果一定是酸的，不能吃，否則，哪輪得到你這樣再三探望，早就淪入旁人的肚腹囉！」

有人說：

「不要以為它的主人遺棄它們！搞不好主人早布下天羅地網，可能曾經有人被抓到，大家口耳相傳，才不敢輕舉妄動。」

於是，大夥兒不約而同地聯想起一位婦人採了幾朵路旁的菊花而被扭送到警察局究辦的新聞，外子於

contest to see which loser would drop first. Although there was no way to count their exact number, they always made me feel dizzy and have hallucinations the moment I looked up. From the end of spring to midsummer, the mangos seemed to have made a pact to hang in there. There were many passer-bys and residents in the neighbourhood. How were they able to survive without ever being disturbed?

Someone said, "It's a no-brainer. Haven't you read a story in the elementary school book? The mangos must be sour and inedible, or else they would have fallen into somebody's stomach long ago without having you check on them constantly."

Another one said, "Don't just assume that the owner has abandoned them. Who knows, maybe it's a trap set by the owner. There was probably someone caught before and the word has spread around. That's why no one dares to act rashly."

As a result, everyone started to recall the news about a woman at the same time. She picked a few chrysanthemums on the roadside, was caught by the owner and taken to the police station. My

是跟兒子、女兒攬功地說：

「我就是這麼想著，要不是我極力攔阻，你媽也許早就上報了！標題我都幫編輯想好了：『偷摘鄰居芒果，某國立大學教授廖×蕙失風被捕』，哎呀！真搞到這種地步，看她怎麼做人！還為人師表哪！」

總之，沒有人同情我，一整個夏天的芒果熱從此降溫，事情彷彿就這麼不了了之。八月初，我們又駕車回中部，我還是忍不住繞道去憑弔一番，誰知，遠遠就看到一樹的芒果集體失蹤，一顆也沒留下，不管樹下或樹上。這回，我只選擇默默驅車離開。

多日之後，學生推薦我們看了德國導演多莉絲朵利（Doris Dorrie）取材自小津安二郎「東京物語」所拍攝的「當櫻花盛開」（Hanami）。描寫一位名叫杜莉的太太，為了遷就丈夫魯迪，忍痛放棄熱愛的

husband then tried to take credit and said to my son and daughter, "That's exactly what I was thinking. If it wasn't for me, your mother would have been in the news long time ago. I even envisioned a headline for the editor: 'Getting caught while stealing neighbour's mango, Professor Liao from So-and-so National University was in custody.' Alas, if things had developed to that stage, how was she going to face the society as well as her students?"

In short, no one was on my side. From then on my mango fever that had lasted the whole summer finally cooled down. Things seemed to come to an end without much ado. When we drove back to Central Taiwan again in early August, I still couldn't help making a detour to the site to ponder the past. But even from a distance I could see there wasn't any mango left, whether on the tree or on the ground. This time, I chose to drive away quietly.

A few days later, we went to see a movie by German director Doris Dorrie at a student's recommendation. The film, *Hanami (Cherry Blossoms)*, was adapted from *Tokyo Story*, a Japanese film directed by Yasujiro Ozu. The story was about a woman named Trudi, who gave up her beloved Japanese traditional dance for

日本傳統舞蹈。丈夫在她過世後，決心完成妻子未竟之夢，飛往日本探視遠在東京工作的小兒子並追尋日本傳統舞蹈精神。他深情地穿上妻子的毛衣、裙子在櫻花盛開的井之頭公園走動，並和因思念母親而在櫻花樹下獨自起舞的小優學習他原先唾棄卻是太太最愛的舞踏。電影終了，當主題曲悠悠響起，全家人還沉浸在哀傷的氣氛中，出乎意料地，外子竟感嘆地跟兒女說：

「唉！也許我不該阻止你媽去摘芒果的，萬一你媽哪天不幸過世，我可能會跟阻止太太跳舞的男主角一樣，後悔不迭地去敲開長芒果樹的人家，然後，站在樹下仰頭對著一樹纍纍的果實嚎啕大哭吧！」

——原載二〇〇九年九月二十五日《聯合報》

收入九歌版《純真遺落》（2009年）

the sake of her husband Rudi. After she passed away, her husband decided to fulfill her unfinished dream. He flew to Japan to visit his youngest son who was working in Tokyo and tried to find the spirit of the Butoh dance. With deep affection in his heart, he put on his wife's sweater and skirt and walked about in the Inokashira Garden among all the cherry blossoms. There he met Yu, who was dancing solo under a cherry tree in memory of her mother, and learned from her his wife's favourite Butoh dance which he had despised earlier. At the end of the movie as the theme music was playing and my family were still immersed in the sad atmosphere, my husband sighed and said to our children out of the blue, "Perhaps I shouldn't have stopped your mother from picking the mangos. Should your mother unfortunately pass away one day, I would probably feel as regretful as the male character that refused to let his wife dance. I would knock open the door of that house with the mango tree and stand under the tree. Looking at the fruit in close clusters above me, I would probably burst into tears."

你不知道我的成績有多爛
You Don't Know How Terrible My Marks Are

胡守芳／譯

Translated by Shou-Fang HU-MOORE

　　她朝我甜蜜溫婉的笑了起來——連她的笑也有蜜柑的味道——她說「啊，你這查某真好，我知，我看就知——」我微笑，沒說話，生意人對顧客總有好話說，可是她仍抓住話題不放……「你真好——你就我少年伊辰一樣——」

天色已暗，微雨中，母子三人在車水馬龍的杭州南路上，焦急的攔車。

每每一部計程車即將行近，就被路邊竄出的人奪得先機。眼見即將誤了搭乘的火車時刻，我再也顧不得禮讓的傳統美德，半跑的追上一部車子，拉開後車門，這時，才發現車子的前座已然坐進一位西裝筆挺的男人。男人很和氣，經過短暫協商，我們決定共乘，車子先行前往火車站，再轉往男子的目的地——新莊。

和陌生人共乘在一個狹小的空間中，是除了乘電梯以外不曾經歷的事，為了感謝他的仁慈，我主動打開話匣子：

「先生在這兒攔車子，是住在這兒嗎？」

The night had already fallen and it was drizzling. With two children by my side, I anxiously watched the heavy traffic on Hangzhou South Road, trying to flag down a taxi.

Every time when one was approaching, it was grabbed by someone darting out from nowhere. Seeing that we were about to miss our train, I could no longer observe the traditional virtue of civility. I ran after a taxi and caught up with it. I pulled the back door open before realizing that the front seat had already been occupied by a well-dressed man in a Western suit. The man was very amicable and, after a brief negotiation, we decided to share the ride. The taxi would take us to the train station first before heading for the man's destination, Xin Zhuang.

Other than in an elevator, riding in a cramped space with a stranger was something I had never done before. In order to show my gratitude for his kindness, I took the step to initiate a conversation.

"Do you live around here, sir, since you flagged down the taxi in this area?"

「不是，我是在這附近上班，金甌女中。」

「老師嗎？還是職員？」

「是校長啦！」

「哇！失敬！失敬！是好鄰居哪！我們就住在你們學校旁。」

一旁靜靜聽著我們對話的女兒，突然興奮起來，對著校長說：「哇！好棒！我媽說，以後我要念你們學校哪！」

半側著身子的校長，和藹的笑著朝女兒說：
「不會的啦！你媽會要你念北一女的啦！」

女兒天真的辯駁道：「你不知道我的成績有多爛！我媽說，我只能念你們學校。是真的！沒騙你。」

"No. I work in the area, in Jin Ou Girls' High School."

"Are you a teacher or a staff member?"

"Well, I am the principal."

"Oh, excuse me for not recognizing you. You are a good neighbour then. We live close to your school."

My daughter who was sitting quietly on the side listening to the conversation suddenly got excited. She said to the principal, "Wow, great! My mom told me that I will attend your school one day."

Turning sideway towards us, the principal affably replied to her with a smile, "No, you won't. Your mom would want you to go to the Taipei First Girls' High School."

My daughter refuted innocently, "You don't know how terrible my marks are! My mom said that I'm only good for your school. It's true! I'm not lying!"

　　我尷尬得不知如何是好，偷偷拉了下女兒的衣袖，示意她不要亂講話，然後，齜牙咧嘴的陪笑道：「沒有啦！小孩子不懂事，亂講話……」

　　女兒回看了我一眼，納悶的問我：「你每次不是都這樣說的嗎？有沒有？有一次在瓊寧家，有沒有？還有……我哪有亂講話！」

　　我羞愧得只差沒從窗口跳出去，校長想是也不知如何面對這個過度誠實的孩子，只咧著嘴呵呵的笑著。幸而車站及時到了，我跟蹌奪門而出，站在暗夜的路邊，忍不住哈哈大笑起來，兩個稚齡的孩子，面面相覷，不知所以，以為媽媽瘋了！

　　這是十年前的往事，那年，女兒剛念國小三年級。事隔七年後，女兒考高中，居然不幸而言中的被

I was embarrassed beyond words and furtively tugged at her sleeve, signalling her to stop babbling. I then put on an awkward smile and said to the principal, "No, no, no. The child knows nothing; she's talking nonsense. ..."

My daughter glanced back at me and asked perplexedly, "Didn't you often say that? Yes or no? Once at Qiong Ning's house, didn't you? And there was another time at?... I'm not talking nonsense!"

I was so embarrassed that I wished I could jump out of the window. Probably not knowing how to deal with this over-honest child either, the principal simply grinned from ear to ear. Fortunately in the nick of time we arrived at the train station. I nearly fell in my flight from the taxi. Standing by the roadside in the darkness, I couldn't help bursting into laughter. My two children looked at each other in bewilderment, probably thinking that their mother had gone mad.

The incident happened ten years ago. My daughter had just started Grade Three that year. Seven years later, she wrote the

分發進了金甌女中。那個下著雨的夜裡，女兒那番天真又讓人尷尬萬分的言語，竟成為生命中奇妙的預言。

開學的第一天，晚飯桌上，女兒興奮的向全家人報告：「今天有校長訓話，哇！還是那位校長哪！臉孔還是跟好多年前一模一樣！完全沒變！真的。」

——原載一九九八年五月二十七日《中國時報》

收入九歌版《沒大沒小》（2009年）

entrance examination to high school and was assigned to Jin Ou Girls' High as she herself had unfortunately foretold. Her innocent, as well as embarrassing, remark on that raining night turned out to be an intriguing self-fulfilling prophecy of her life.

At the dinner table on the first day of school, she reported to the whole family in great excitement, "The principal gave a speech today. Wow, that man is still the principal! His face looks exactly the same as many years ago. He's totally unchanged, honest!"

情深似海
Ocean-deep Affection

胡守芳／譯

Translated by Shou-Fang HU-MOORE

　　女兒很認真地併攏腳跟，無限深情地說：「我媽媽說你是她最好的朋友，謝謝你以前那麼照顧我媽。」一股熱氣往腦門兒直衝了上去，我喉嚨驀地哽咽了起來，眼睛霎時又溼又熱，我束手無策，萬萬沒想到女兒竟會如此做。朋友的眼睛也陡地紅了起來，嘴脣微顫，卻是一句話也說不出來，只緊緊摟過女兒。

暑假期間，一位昔日好友由倫敦回來。我們約在信義路金石堂五樓的咖啡屋中見面。

夏日的午後，鬱熱難當，我拉著女兒的手，走在人潮滾滾的街道上，覺得整個城市似乎要燃燒起來。女兒的小手，常因逆向行走的行人的衝撞而由我手中鬆脫，然而，很快地，又會迎上前來。我們就在商家框喝聲、行人討價還價聲中，斷斷續續地聊著。

女兒問我即將和什麼人見面，我說：「是媽媽大學畢業後留在學校當助教時的同事，由很遠的英國回來。」

女兒側著頭天真地問：「是不是從很遠的地方回來的人，都要約著見面，請他們喝咖啡？」

During the summer break, an old friend of mine came back from London. We made a date to meet at the coffee shop on the fifth floor of Eslite Bookstore on Xinyi Road.

The sweltering summer afternoon was unbearably hot. Holding hands with my daughter, I walked on streets crowded with people and felt the entire city was about to be on fire. As the oncoming pedestrian traffic brushed against us, my daughter's little hand slipped off now and then but quickly came back to seek mine again. We carried a conversation off and on in the midst of the haggling over merchandise on the street.

My daughter asked me whom I was going to meet. I told her, "A colleague of mine from the university where I stayed on as a teaching assistant after graduation. She came back from Britain, a place very far away."

My daughter tilted her head and asked innocently, "Do you always have to meet people from far-away places and invite them for coffee?"

「那倒不一定啦！媽媽那時候同她感情最好，一起做助教時，她很照顧媽媽。」

女兒鍥而不舍地接著問：「大人也還要人家照顧嗎？她怎麼照顧你？是不是像蔡和純照顧我一樣？教你做功課？」

蔡和純是她的同班同學。我聽了不由得笑了起來說：「大概差不多吧！人再大，也需要別人照顧呀！對不對？像爺爺生病了，也要我們照顧嘛！對不對？……」

「那你生病了嗎？那時候。」

「生病倒沒有。不過，那年，有一段時間，媽媽的心情很不好，覺得自己很討人嫌，人緣很差。就在那年聖誕節前幾天，我發現王阿姨偷偷地在我辦公桌

"It's not always the case. She was Mommy's best friend when we were both working as teaching assistants. She looked after Mommy a lot."

My daughter continued her questioning persistently, "Do adults also need someone to look after them? How did she look after you? Was it like the way that Cai Hechun looks after me? Did she help you with homework?"

Cai Hechun was her classmate. Amused by her words, I couldn't but laugh while replying, "It's probably similar. Even a grown-up needs someone to look after him. Isn't it so? For instance, if Grandpa gets sick, he will also need us to look after him. Isn't it right? …"

"Then, were you sick at the time?"

"No, I wasn't sick. But, back then there was a period of time when Mommy was in a bad mood. I had poor relations with others and felt disliked. But just a few days prior to Christmas that year, I found a greeting card on my desk in the office. It was hand made

上夾了張她自己做的賀卡，上面寫著：『我不知道怎樣形容我有多麼喜歡你，祝你佳節愉快。』媽媽看了好感動。這張卡片改變了當時媽媽惡劣的心情。更重要的是，給了我很大的鼓勵，使我覺得自己並不那麼討厭！」

女兒聽了，若有所思，低頭不語。

我和朋友見了面，開心地談著往事、彼此探問著現況，女兒一旁安靜地聽著，不像往常般吱吱喳喳搶著說，我們幾乎忘了她的存在。

一會兒工夫後，女兒要求到三樓文具部去看看。十分鐘後，女兒紅著臉，氣喘吁吁地上樓來，朝我悄悄地說：「先借給我一百元好嗎？我想買一個東西，回去再從撲滿拿錢還你。」

by Auntie Wong, in which she wrote, 'I don't know how to tell you that I really like you. Have a good Christmas holiday!' Mommy was very touched. The card changed my frame of mind. More importantly, it boosted my spirit, making me feel not too bad about myself."

After hearing that, my daughter seemed to be deep in thought and lowered her head without saying anything.

After my friend and I met, we chatted cheerfully about old times and inquired about each other's current situation. Unlike her old self, who often butted in to make comments, my daughter sat listening on the side so quietly that we almost forgot her presence.

After a while, my daughter asked for permission to go down to the stationery section on the third floor for a look. Ten minutes later, she came back red-faced, panting hard from climbing the stairs. She said to me in a whisper, "Can I borrow one hundred dollars from you now? I want to buy something. I'll pay you back with money in my piggy bank when we get home."

　　我和同學談得高興，無暇細想，知她不會亂花錢，便拿錢打發她。過沒多久，她又上來了。面對朋友，恭敬地立正，雙手捧上一盒包裝精美的禮物，一派正經地說：「王阿姨！送你一個小禮物，你從那麼遠的地方回來。」

　　朋友和我同時大吃了一驚，朋友手足無措，訥訥地說：「那怎麼行！我怎麼能收你的禮物！……我從英國回來，沒帶禮物給你，已經很不好意思了，而且，我是大人，你是小孩兒……」

　　女兒很認真地併攏腳跟，無限深情地說：「我媽媽說你是她最好的朋友，謝謝你以前那麼照顧我媽。」

　　一股熱氣往腦門兒直衝了上去，我喉嚨驀地哽咽了起來，眼睛霎時又溼又熱，我束手無策，萬萬沒想

Deep in a pleasant conversation with my friend, I didn't give her request much thought. Knowing that she wouldn't spend recklessly, I dismissed her by giving her the money. In a short while, she was back again. Facing my friend, she stood at attention to show respect and offered her a well-wrapped gift with both hands. She said to her very seriously, "Auntie Wong, here is a small gift for you. You came back from such a far-away place."

My friend and I were both stunned. Not knowing how to react, my friend spoke hesitantly, "No way! How can I accept your gift? ... I've already felt quite guilty that I didn't bring you any gift from Britain. Besides, I'm an adult and you're a child. ..."

My daughter drew her heels together in earnest and spoke with deep affection, "My mom said that you are her best friend. Thank you for looking after my mom in the past."

A hot torrent rushed into my brain. All of a sudden there was a lump in my throat and my eyes felt warm and moist. Having never imagined that my daughter would do such a thing, I was at a loss

到女兒竟會如此做。朋友的眼睛也陡地紅了起來，嘴唇微顫，卻是一句話也說不出來，只緊緊摟過女兒，喃喃說道：「謝謝啊！謝謝……」

這回輪到女兒覺得不好意思了。她伏在朋友肩上尷尬地提醒朋友：「你想不想看看你得到什麼禮物啊？」

朋友拆開禮物，是掛了個毛絨絨小白兔的鑰匙圈。女兒老氣橫秋地說：「會照顧人的人一定是很溫柔的，所以，我選了小白兔，白白軟軟的，你喜歡嗎？」

朋友感動的說：「當然喜歡了，好可愛的禮物。我回英國去，就把所有的鑰匙都掛上，每打開一扇門，就想一次你。……真謝謝啊……」

what to do. The eyes of my friend suddenly turned red, too. Her lips quivered but couldn't utter a word. She simply held her tightly in her arms and muttered, "Thank you. Thank you…"

My daughter in turn felt rather embarrassed by this. Leaning against my friend's shoulder, she tried awkwardly to remind her, "Do you want to see what I got you?"

My friend opened the package and saw a key-ring with a pendant of a little downy rabbit. My daughter spoke in a tone of an elder to her, "People who look after others must be very soft and gentle. Therefore, I chose a little rabbit with white and soft fur for you. Do you like it?"

My friend was deeply moved and replied, "Of course I like it. What a lovely gift it is. After I go back to Britain, I'm going to attach all my keys to it. Every time I unlock a door, I will be thinking of you. …Thank you so much. …"

女兒高興得又蹦又跳地下樓去了，留下兩個女人
在飄著咖啡香的屋裡領受著比咖啡還要香醇的情誼。

———原載一九九一年二月三日《中華日報》

收入九歌版《不信溫柔喚不回》（2006年）

My daughter was so happy that she skipped all the way downstairs, leaving the two women in the room permeated with the aroma of coffee to savour their friendship that was even stronger and sweeter than coffee.

像我這樣的老師
A Teacher Like Me

胡守芳／譯

Translated by Shou-Fang HU-MOORE

像我這樣的老師，因為很知道自己的弱點，所以，總是使盡了吃奶的力氣務求不二過，然而，人間的事實在太複雜，縱然從不二過，不斷翻新的失誤也絕對足夠讓生活多姿多彩、驚心動魄。譬如一些幾近靈異事件，若非親身經歷，鐵定無法想像。一回脫蓋又漏水的紅墨筆居然氾濫成災，將計分冊上所登錄的分數徹底淹沒了好幾個。幸賴學生誠實回報，否則還真沒辦法收拾善後。

**像我這樣的老師，忘性比記性快數十倍，精明
比糊塗少幾百分，看起來優遊自在，其實成天
提心吊膽。**

值得擔心的事實在太多：萬一考卷遺失、如果分數
算錯、倘設計分簿忘了擱在何處、如果導生出了車
禍⋯⋯每一個環節都潛藏無法預料的危機，難怪失眠
症候尾隨不去。午夜夢迴，經常驚出一身冷汗。說實
在的，能教二十餘年書，還沒有犯太嚴重的過失或提
前被學校解聘，真是託天之幸。

　　像我這樣的老師，帶錯課本、走錯教室，幾乎無
「週」不有之。幸而師生雙方已培養出相當的默契：
老師在家勤於備課、絞盡腦汁提醒自己自愛；學生群
裡，學長傳學弟、學姊叮嚀學妹，代代相傳，知道老
師的糊塗，寬容加體貼，也早早備好應對良方。上課

A teacher like me forgets ten times faster than she can remember, and her astuteness lags behind her obtuseness by hundreds of points.

I appear to be carefree and at ease, but in fact am anxious all the time. There are too many things to worry about, such as: what if the examination papers got lost, the students' marks were miscalculated, the record of their marks was misplaced or a student of mine got into a car accident, and so on. There are unpredictable crises hidden everywhere; no wonder insomnia follows me around. I often wake up in the middle of the night in a cold sweat. To be honest, it is truly God's grace that I have been able to teach for over twenty years without making too serious a mistake or having my teaching post prematurely terminated.

For a teacher like me, hardly a week passes without seeing me bring the wrong textbook or walk into the wrong classroom. Fortunately a tacit understanding has been established between the teacher and students. The teacher diligently prepares the lessons at home and keeps vigilance on her own behaviour to show self-respect. Knowing how absent-minded the teacher is, the students have been passing advice from seniors to juniors to be tolerant

前，派員到研究室內拘捕教授是一種；上課五分鐘後，分頭到各樓層追緝是另一種；幫老師多預備一本課本是基本常識；隨機奉上原子筆或衛生紙是尋常小事；帶爸媽的老花眼鏡來讓老師備用則是分外的體貼；下課後，送回老師遺忘在教室內的外套則是冬日的額外服務。幸而，雖然狀況頻傳，倒無重大到不可收拾的情事發生。

像我這樣的老師，必須坦白招認，儘管一直兢兢業業、深自惕勵，卻只能勉強維持大事不犯，小過可是從來不斷。記憶深刻的幾次幾乎被嚇破膽的事，都跟考卷脫離不了干係。十餘年前，一個下著毛毛細雨的午後。考完試，開車繞進家裡的小巷內，抱著厚厚一疊考卷從車裡出來，驀地一陣旋風直撲巷底，居

and considerate, and have also figured out strategies to deal with the matter. One of them is to send someone to the faculty office "to pick the teacher up" before class. Another one is to search all the floors for "the suspect" when the class should have started five minutes ago. It is a common knowledge to have an extra textbook ready for the teacher. Passing a ball-point pen or tissue paper to the teacher when needed is but a regular minor matter. Exceptional considerateness is shown when a student brings his parents' reading glasses to class just in case the teacher should need them. An extra service in the winter is to retrieve the teacher's coat left behind in the classroom. Fortunately, despite the high frequency of accidents, there hasn't been one too disastrous to handle.

A teacher like me must confess that, despite being conscientiously cautious all the time, I only manage to avoid catastrophes, not small errors. Several incidents that have left a deep impression and scared me to death are all related to examination papers. One drizzling afternoon over ten years ago, I drove into the alley near home after giving students an examination. While I was getting out of the car with a stack of examination papers, a whirlwind suddenly hit the alley and swept away all the papers in my arms. Sheets of

然將我手上的考卷席捲而去。就這樣，考卷像鵝毛般一張張四下飛舞，我的魂魄也隨之飛上了天。驚嚇之餘，我拔足狂奔，雙手往天空胡亂抓取，巷內幾位正冒著雨玩耍的小朋友見狀，心花怒放地當成追逐遊戲。一時之間，巷內氣氛為之沸騰，有位小朋友光顧著追考卷，一不小心撞上了牆，哇哇大哭了起來；大部分的小朋友像是遇到嘉年華會似的，對著飛舞的紙張拍手歡呼。雨越下越大，眼見幾張考卷飄呀飄地飄過圍牆，就那樣丰姿綽約地落進了一家無人應門的院內。情急生智，當下發出緊急懸賞——一張考卷十元，雖非重賞，卻立即有小勇夫一位報名，身手矯健地翻牆進去，找回了四張濕淋淋的卷子。雖然因為雨水的洗滌，考卷面目有些模糊，但是，對那位見「利」勇為的小朋友，倒真是叩頭如倒蒜，感謝他臨危受命，恩同再造。

　　像我這樣的老師，真是可憐！雖然只是虛驚一

paper danced and flew in the air like loose feathers, and my soul seemed to have also left my body. I was in a panic and immediately gave chase with my hands stretched high up in the air, gripping and grabbing. Several children playing in the alley at the time saw the situation. Thinking it was a game, they joined the pursuit excitedly. All of a sudden, the atmosphere in the alley heated up. One of the children was so absorbed in the paper chase that he ran into the wall and started bawling. Most of the children clapped and cheered at the flying papers as if they were at a carnival. The rain came down harder and harder. I caught sight of a few sheets gracefully flying over an enclosed wall into the yard of a house where no one was at home. I got an idea in the moment of desperation, urgently offering a reward for ten dollars per sheet. It wasn't a sizable prize, but a brave little man came forward right away to volunteer. He nimbly climbed over the wall and retrieved four wet sheets for me. Although the writing on the examination papers was blurred by the raindrops, I feel forever and ever indebted to the boy who rushed to my rescue, albeit for gain not justice.

A teacher like me is really pathetic. Although there wasn't

場，但從那以後，我每回攜帶考卷，總不忘用數條橡皮筋將它再三綑紮，並緊緊攬在懷裡。這件事的後患無窮，從那之後，漫天飛舞的考卷直攻夢境，取代了纏繞不休的寫不出答案的聯考噩夢，我變得神經兮兮的。

烏龍事當然不止這一樁，另有一件讓我耿耿於懷十餘年的事，也是和考卷相關的。

一回，將成績登錄完畢後，發現有一位學生既未請假，也沒考卷。像我這樣認真負責的老師自然不敢掉以輕心，趕緊一通電話打到宿舍內問明緣由。電話那一頭傳來篤定的回答：

「報告教授！我去考試了呀。」

這年頭，學生的花樣可多了！我才不會輕易上

any real harm done in the incident, I have since always carefully wrapped several elastic bands around the examination papers and held them tightly against my chest while carrying them. There is no end to the aftermath either. Since then, my dreams have been taken over by examination papers flying in the air, replacing an earlier haunting nightmare in which my brain froze while writing the entrance exam to university. I have become a complete nervous wreck.

This certainly is not my only blunder. Another incident haunting me for more than a decade is also related to examination papers.

Once, after recording the students' marks, I noticed that the examination paper of a student who wasn't on leave was missing. Being an earnest and responsible teacher, I certainly dared not treat the matter lightly. I immediately made a phone call to the students' dormitory to find out the reason. From the other end of the line came a confident reply, "Professor, I did write the exam."

Students can play all kinds of tricks these days and I won't be

當！上次有位學生沒繳作文還硬拗，害得缺乏信心的我自責地找了又找，其後在教師休息室裡偶然和其他教授相互切磋，才發現這位學生前科累累，慣用這樣栽贓的方式逃避繳交作業。

「我可是經驗老到的！想用這樣的老套！哼！去騙其他的菜鳥老師吧！我精得跟水晶猴子似的！想騙我？門兒都沒有。」

我心裡這樣小人地陰陰想著，表面上沒忘記維持民主的風範：

「你說你來考了，我卻沒看到你的考卷，這個事情可麻煩大了！……這樣吧！我也不為難你，你若真的出席考試，必然有同學看到你，你就找個同學來作證吧。」

easily duped. There was previously a student who didn't hand in a composition but kept insisting that he did. Lacking confidence in myself, I ended up blaming myself and searched everywhere for it. Later on, after a casual conversation with other professors in the office, I discovered that this student had a record of evading homework by using similar tactics of putting the blame on others.

"I am certainly well experienced now. This kind of old trick can only fool the inexperienced new teachers. I am just as astute as a 'crystal monkey'[1]. Don't even think about deceiving me."

I thought to myself guilefully. But I kept a democratic demeanour on the surface and said, "You said that you wrote the exam, but I don't have your paper. This creates a big problem. ... Let's do it this way. I won't make it difficult for you. If you did attend the exam, other students must have seen you there. Find a classmate to bear witness for you."

1.——*A crystal monkey in Chinese refers to a person of cunning and deceitful character.*

電話掛斷沒多久，證人打電話來了，他說他可以證明當事人曾經來考試。

「那你看到他繳卷了嗎？」

他一時語塞，沒說話。我乘勝追擊，警告他做偽證是犯法的！到時候被揭發了，將吃不完兜著走！我侃侃而談，從道德、法律、人情三方面展開勸說，結論是：

「老師知道你想為朋友兩肋插刀，效古之俠者！但是是非不分地出來幫忙作偽證，不但是姑息養奸，也不是一位真正的好朋友該做的事。……我再鄭重地問你一次：你真的看到他繳卷了嗎？」

支支吾吾的，電話那頭囁嚅地說：
「我是看到他來考試，……可是，沒……沒看到他繳卷。」

Shortly after I hung up, I got a phone call from his witness. He said he could testify that his classmate was present at the examination.

"Then, did you see him hand in the examination paper?"

He became tongue-tied and didn't answer. I seized the opportunity to pursue it further, warning him that it was a criminal offense to bear false witness. Should it be exposed, he would be in big trouble. I spoke with fervour and confidence, trying to persuade him on moral, legal and emotional grounds. I concluded by saying, "I know you want to follow the chivalrous examples of ancient heroes, helping your friend in time of need. But if you don't tell right from wrong and help him by bearing false witness, you are not only abetting evil by tolerating it, but doing something that a true friend shouldn't do. ... Let me ask you one more time seriously: did you actually see him handing in the paper?"

The voice at the other end of the line wavered, "I did see him at the exam, ... but I cannot say I saw him hand in the paper."

　　我心裡暗暗鬆了一口氣！學生終究還是天真無邪的，沒敢說謊到底、鑄成大錯。證人將電話交給那位嫌疑犯，嫌疑犯嘟嘟囔囔的，在電話那頭和證人抗議著。我義正辭嚴地再問一次：

　　「沒來考試事小，就算考了試後，覺得成績不理想沒繳卷，都不算大事，最糟糕的是，被發現了，還不承認！殺人也不過頭點地，知錯能改，老師不會趕盡殺絕、不給你機會的，你好好想想！……我最後再問你一次：你真的繳了考卷嗎？」

　　「如果教授說沒繳，那就沒繳吧！」

　　雖然覺得學生的態度不是太理想，但是，想來也是一時之間難以從容下臺階吧！學生嘛！只要肯承認錯誤，就不要逼他太甚了！我沾沾自喜處置得宜，總算沒讓失足學生一錯再錯。

I breathed a sigh of relief to myself. The student was artless and naive after all. He didn't commit a gross mistake by insisting on lying. "The witness" handed the phone to "the suspect" and "the suspect" mumbled something to "the witness" in protest. I asked him one more time sternly out of a sense of justice, "It's nothing serious if you didn't attend the exam. Nor would it be a problem if you didn't hand in the paper because you felt that you didn't do well at the exam. The worst thing is that you won't admit it after being exposed. This is not a murder case. If you know that you did something wrong and make amends for it, I won't be so ruthless as to deprive you of a second chance. You'd better give it a good thought. … I'll ask you for the last time: did you hand in the exam paper?"

"Professor, if you say that I didn't, then I didn't."

Although I felt the student's attitude wasn't as good as I expected, it was probably because he couldn't find a way to back down gracefully for the moment. After all, he's only a student. As long as he admits the mistake, I won't force him into a corner. I was pleased with myself for handling the matter well so that a student who made a mistake wouldn't continue to make further mistakes.

第二天，來清掃的歐巴桑搬開厚重龐大的沙發，赫然清出一張考卷，我見了差點兒沒暈死過去，考卷上頭端端正正寫著那名嫌疑犯的名字！如果我尚且有些許道德勇氣，應該一頭撞死的。可我貪生怕死，沒那樣做。經過一夜輾轉無眠，次日，我黑著眼圈，拿著考卷，找來那位同學，跟他說：

「考卷終於找到了！為甚麼你昨天沒堅持到底？明明繳了卷，為甚麼最後還承認你沒繳？」

同學低著頭，無可奈何地說：

「那我能怎麼辦？我說我去考試了，你說沒有；我說我繳卷了，你說你沒看到卷子，而我那位同學又不顧道義，不肯還我清白。我能怎麼辦！只好⋯⋯」

於是，我又花了好多時間跟他說明道德勇氣的重要，闡述「吾愛吾師，吾更愛真理」的至理名言，強

The following day, as my cleaning lady lifted up the huge heavy sofa in my house to clean the floor, she discovered an examination paper. When I saw it, I nearly fainted. The name of "the suspect" was neatly written on it. If there was any moral courage left in me, I should have rammed my head into the wall to kill myself. But I cared too much for my own life and didn't do it. After a sleepless night, I took the paper to school with dark rims around my eyes, and found the accused student. I said to him, "I've found your paper. Why didn't you insist on your innocence to the end yesterday? Obviously you did hand in the exam paper. Why in the end did you profess that you didn't?"

The student lowered his head and replied helplessly, "What could I do? I said that I wrote the exam, but you said I didn't. I said that I handed in the paper, but you said that you didn't see it. That classmate of mine wouldn't stand firmly on the moral ground to clear my name. What could I do? I could only…"

As a result, I spent a lot of time explaining to him about the importance of moral courage, expounding on Aristotle's famous dictum: "Plato is dear to me, but dearer still is truth", and stressing

調卓爾不群、抗拒強權的修持是革命青年的必修，說著、說著，紅了眼眶：

「那現在怎麼辦？你陷老師於不義！害老師必須跟你道歉！……對不起啦！冤枉了你！老師也會犯錯的哪！你不要生氣好嗎？」

學生慌了手腳，急急說道：

「老師不要這樣！考卷找到就好了，我怎麼會生老師的氣！都是我不好，沒有堅持做對的事，對不起老師。」

「那我們算扯平了？」

我破涕為笑，漫天烏雲化為烏有。從那以後，我不但謹守考試點名的規範，而且養成每改完一次卷子必清掃沙發下的習慣。

that a youth of progressive spirit must cultivate independent thinking and stand firm against authorities. As I carried on and on, my eyes started to turn red, "What should I do now? You led your teacher into in a moral quandary. Now I have to apologize to you. ... I'm sorry for having wronged you. Even a teacher can make mistake. Don't be angry with me, O.K.?"

The student became flustered and hastily replied, "Don't do this, Professor. Now that you have found my paper, everything is fine. I won't be angry with you. It's my fault that I didn't insist on doing the right thing. I'm sorry, Professor."

"Then we can call it even now,"

I broke into a smile through tears. All the dark clouds disappeared. From then on, I not only strictly carry out the routine of roll-call at every examination, but have also developed the habit of sweeping the underside of the sofa every time I finish marking the papers.

像我這樣的老師，因為很知道自己的弱點，所以，總是使盡了吃奶的力氣務求不二過，然而，人間的事實在太複雜，縱然從不二過，不斷翻新的失誤也絕對足夠讓生活多姿多彩、驚心動魄。譬如一些幾近靈異事件，若非親身經歷，鐵定無法想像。一回脫蓋又漏水的紅墨筆居然氾濫成災，將計分冊上所登錄的分數徹底淹沒了好幾個。幸賴學生誠實回報，否則還真沒辦法收拾善後。在這之前，我完全不知道紅墨水的腐蝕性如此之強，在那之後，我終於找到除了王水之外的另類殺人滅跡滴劑。

一年前，因為重新整修屋子，我們清掉了大批舊東西，衣服、書報、雜誌、書信……丟到眼睛泛紅、心裡發狠，只差沒腦袋抓狂。半夜醒來，不知怎地，忽然記起一包剛剛考完、尚未批閱的期中考卷。腦子一陣發暈，急忙起身尋找，越找越慌，急急將外子由夢中搖醒，一口咬定：

Since a teacher like me knows her own weakness, I always try my best not to make the same mistake twice. However, things are too complicated in life. Even though I never make the same mistake twice, constant new blunders continue to make my life interesting as well as scary. For instance, some of the near-occult incidents would be very difficult to imagine if I didn't go through the experience myself. Once my red-ink pen lost its cap and the ink flooded my mark-book, wiping out the record of several students' marks. Fortunately those students reported their marks to me again honestly, or else the situation would have been quite difficult to handle. Before the incident, I was totally unaware of the "corrosive" power of red ink. Afterwards, I think I finally found an alternative "killer-fluid" besides Aqua Regia.

A year ago, in the process of renovating our home, we threw away a lot of old things, such as clothes, newspapers, magazines, letters and so on. I went into a frenzy disposing of so many things that my mind seemed to have also been tossed away. One night I woke up and suddenly remembered a bag of mid-term examination papers that was yet to be marked. I felt giddy all at once and got up immediately to look for it. As I was searching, I became more and

「一定是被你收拾進前一天綑紮丟掉的報紙堆中了！我就知道！這下子完蛋了。」

外子從睡夢中被吵醒，乍然聽到這樣的指控，也嚇得魂不附體。夜深人靜，我們發瘋似地打開所有的燈光，找遍了每一個角落，就差沒把地板掀開了。靈光一現，外子說：

「我昨晚丟舊書報雜誌時，正好遇到里長。他讓我放前門邊兒，不必送去資源回收車，就等他明日一起處理。也許他還沒扔掉！我下去看看。」

於是，夫妻二人像個夜賊，鬼鬼祟祟帶著手電筒下樓。書報雜誌竟然仍整整齊齊堆在那兒！我們欣喜若狂，顧不得形象，像覓食的狗兒一般，在門前行人

more panicked and hurriedly woke my husband up. I accused him assertively, "It must have been put into the stack of newspapers that you tied up and threw away yesterday. I just know it. Now I'm done for."

Woken from sleep, my husband was scared out of his wits to hear this sudden accusation. In the middle of the night, we frantically turned on all the lights searching every corner, only short of pulling the floor boards up. Suddenly something dawned on my husband and he said, "While taking out the old newspapers and magazines last night, I bumped into the head of our neighbourhood. He asked me to leave them by the front door. He said there was no need for me to take them to the recycling truck, because he was going to take care of them tomorrow with other stuff. Perhaps he hasn't taken them yet. Let me go downstairs to have a look."

As a result, we sneaked downstairs with a torch like a pair of thieves and found the newspapers and magazines were still in a neat pile there. We were so elated that we could care less how we looked and started rummaging through the pile on the sidewalk like two

道的廢物堆上翻來找去，然而，終究只是徒勞。像洩了氣的皮球，怏怏然上樓，我們像楚囚般對著嘆氣到黎明。而因為我先發制人，所以，外子便倒楣地成了低姿態的兇嫌，欲辯已忘言。

第二天，等不到天亮，二人分頭奔走：外子直奔工作室，我驅車前往研究室。翻箱倒櫃了半日，互通電話，咸感絕望。我愣坐研究室內，開始做最壞的打算。怎麼辦？承認錯誤，全班再考一次？雖然誠實的德行可以媲美砍伐櫻桃樹的華盛頓，但缺乏豐功偉績，只怕劣跡再添一樁，這樣的糊塗帳將會被歷屆學生傳頌千古、永世不得超生，嗯，不妥！要麼，乾脆耍個機心，佯裝氣惱全班都考得太差，老師再給一次重考機會！不好！做人豈可如此顛倒是非、厚顏無恥。那麼，假裝汽車遭竊，考卷隨之灰飛煙滅？咦？汽車？……我腦中閃過一個念頭，整個人像裝了彈簧般彈起來，飛快往停車場奔去。拉開行李箱，天可憐

dogs looking for food. But, in the end it was all in vain. We went back upstairs discouraged like deflated rubber balls and sat there sighing and moaning till daybreak. Since I was the one who gained the upper hand by striking first, my husband could only stoop low as an unlucky "suspect" without a word to defend himself.

Before the sun rose the next day, we each went our separate way. He ran straight to his studio and I drove to my office. After turning the space upside down for another half day, we called each other in disappointment. I sat in my office and started to prepare for the worst. What should I do? Should I admit the mistake and get the whole class to write another exam? Although being honest could win me merit rivalling George Washington who chopped down a cherry tree by mistake in his youth, I lack the great achievements that he had. I'm afraid it would only be another misdeed on my record. The story of my blunder would be passed down from generation to generation among the students till eternity. That's not good. Or, maybe I should pull a trick, pretending to be upset that the whole class didn't do well at the exam and to show meray by giving them a chance to write another exam. That's not good either. How could I be so shameless as to

見！考卷正蜷曲著身子躲在那兒哪！原來，前一天為了幾位搭便車的乘客，我順手將放在座位上的考卷放進行李箱了。那天晚上，我輕手輕腳回到家，前所未有的腰軟嘴甜、斜肩諂媚，外子寒著臉哼哼冷笑，說：

「你不該姓廖，該姓賴！……哼！怎麼會有像你這樣的老師！」

——原載二○○四年二月十四日《聯合報》

收入九歌版《像我這樣的老師》（2004年）

distort the truth! Then, maybe I could pretend that my car was stolen and the examination papers disappeared with it. Hey, my car? ... A thought suddenly flashed across my mind. I sprang up from my seat and dashed towards the parking lot. I opened the trunk of my car. Goodness gracious! The bag of examination papers was lying inside. It turned out to be that the day before, in order to give several people a lift, I took the bag of papers on the car seat and put it in the trunk without thinking. I sneaked into the house quietly that evening and fawned on my husband with sweet talk and charm that I had never used before. Pulling a long face, he sneered and said, "Your last name should not be Liao. It should be LAI[2]! ... For Heaven's sake, how can there be a teacher like you!"

2.——— *Chinese family name LAI can also be used in other context and have several different meanings. One of them is "to put the blame on somebody else". Another is "to deny one' s error or responsibility".*

遠　方

In the Distance

謝孟宗／譯

Translated by Meng-Tsung Hsieh

　　母親走了，不知去了何方！兒子緊接著遠走他鄉！去到我沒辦法想像的南美洲，而我也糊裡糊塗接到新學校的聘書，即將變換跑道。一張張學生致贈的卡片，寫滿了捨不得我離開的字句，讓我閱之肝腸寸斷。幾個重大的變化接踵而至，攪得我手忙腳亂，心裡亂糟糟。

在電子業工作四年餘，業績正臻高峰，前途一片看好之際，兒子忽然萌生「棄業」之思。

他說：

「工作太累了！夙夜匪懈這麼久，我想辭職休息一陣子。」

「四年多叫『久』？有沒有搞錯！你老媽我自投入職場以來，今年堂堂邁入三十年，從來也沒想到過可以辭職休息，怎麼平平是人，命運差得這麼多！」我哀怨地嘀咕著。

「你不同！你當教授，工時短，寒暑假又有兩、三個月可以休息，哪像我們日也操、暝也操，一刻不得閒。……更可怕的是，竟然我好像對眼前的工作越來越適應，似乎一輩子就可以這樣子過下去了！可是，實在不甘心啊，我的一生難道就該這樣決定了嗎？……依照你們的期待娶妻、生子，或朝九晚五，

Having worked in the electronic industry for over four years, with a top sales record and a bright prospect, my boy all of a sudden thought of giving up his career. He said, "My job is too tiring. I have worked hard by day and by night for so long, and I would like to take a rest for a while. "

"You call 'over four years' long! Are you serious! This year marks the thirtieth anniversary of my being a career woman, and I have never thought of quitting and taking some rest. Oh, how people's destinies differ!" I grumbled like a bitter old mom.

"Your case is different! You are a college professor, enjoying short working hours and having winter, have summer vacations of two to three months. People like me have to work really hard by day and by night, not having a single moment to spare. What's worse, it seems that I am getting increasingly used to my present job and that I can spend my whole life on it! But, honestly, I am not willing to do this. Is this what my life should be, getting married and starting a family as you and dad have always wanted,

或無日無夜坐飛機在各國的旅館間穿梭往來？」

我急急撇清：

「我可沒期待你娶妻、生子，抱不抱孫子我一點也不介意！一切都請自行負責，不要『牽拖』！」

「我想辭職到中南美洲去好好思考我的人生！」他眼神縹緲卻語氣堅定。

從潭子到台北養病已一段時日的外婆，坐在一旁聽了半晌，也興奮起來，她想出兩全其美之計：

「要思考人生，敢不行佇厝內或是去比較近的所在去思考？潭子我那間厝，闊隆隆，汝要安怎去想都可以，無人會吵汝，順便去幫我澆澆花，極久無轉去，恐驚我種的那些蘭花都死了了！」

working from nine o'clock in the morning to five o'clock in the afternoon, or taking business trips on the plane, not knowing whether it's daytime or nighttime, and staying in different hotels around the world?"

Hurriedly I explained, "I have never wanted to push you to get married and start a family. I don't care whether I have grandchildren or not! It's your business. Don't blame me for any decisions you make!"

"I would like to quit my job and go to the Central and South Americas, where I can think carefully about my life!" His eyes were vague, but his voice was firm.

Having been listening to our conversation for a while, my boy's granny, who had moved from Tanzi and stayed in Taipei for some time to recover from her illness, got all excited and came up with some idea she thought would satisfy all parties: "Can't you stay home or somewhere nearby to think about what you wanna do with your life? Boy, you can stay in my house in Tanzi. That house sure is huge, and you can think all you want about what you wanna

兒子聽了大笑起來！哄著外婆說：

「阿嬤！你的花，我會找時間回去澆水啦！不會死啦！您不用操心。」

為什麼選擇中南美？不選擇比較先進一點的歐美國家？兒子有一番奇異的說辭：

「我想藉由你們老人家看似危險、年輕人欣羨的壯遊，將自己抽離習慣的舒適環境，強迫學習獨立生活的能力，藉此克服內心的恐懼，並思考未來的下一步該怎麼走，這叫『一兼二顧，摸蛤兼洗褲』。何況，中南美的奇險壯麗不是很吸引人嗎？」

do for your future. No one's gonna bother you. And when you're there, water my flowers for me, will you? I haven't been there for a long time, and I am afraid my orchids have all withered by now."

My boy laughed really hard after hearing what his granny said. He said soothingly, "Granny, I will find some time to water your flowers. I won't let them wither away. There is no need to worry about it."

As to why my boy decided to go to the Central and South Americas, instead of the more advanced European countries, well, he had some peculiar reason of his own: "This grand tour of mine, which is bound to scare old people like you and at the same time fill the young with envy, will yank me from the comfortable environment I am used to and force me to learn independent living skills. With this tour I hope to conquer my fears and think about what my next step in life should be. As the Taiwanese saying goes, 'Washing your pants while collecting clams in the water, you fulfill two purposes at once.' Besides, don't the Central and South Americans boast some of the most spectacular landscapes in the world?"

　　我以為兒子自小天不怕、地不怕的，竟然說要藉「壯遊」來壯膽，我雖然覺得他的理由太官方，但他一向超有主見，一旦決定的事，非常不容易被說服，與其大費唇舌和他做無謂的爭論，不如乾脆順水推舟，至少可以贏得「孝子」（孝順兒子）的美名。何況我私心裡也挺羨慕他的機緣與壯舉，於是，只好訕笑著說：

　　「好啦！既然決定了，就放心去吧！我和爸爸都支持你。你先去，如果覺得不錯，我們也跟著過去思考我們往後有限的人生吧！」

　　就這樣，兒子的中南美之行算是拍板定案。

　　接著，遞辭呈。早就風聞的老闆百般勸阻、軟硬兼施，最後，眼看勢不可擋，甚至還慷慨允諾給他長時間的假期，但兒子豪邁地說：

　　「做人要顧道義，自己愛玩，不能拖著公司下

My boy had been afraid of nothing since he was a kid, and now he talked about conquering his fears with this grand tour of his. Although his reason seemed too politically correct, I decided to stand with him, not against him, and at least in this way fulfill "parental piety" towards my boy. After all, I thought, my boy had always been very determined, and it would be very difficult to dissuade him from something he had decided on. Besides, in my heart of hearts, I envied that he had such an opportunity to achieve something magnificent. So, I said to him, laughing, "Alright, since you have made up you mind, just do it, and your dad and I will support you. Well, go ahead, and if things turn out well, we will follow you there and think about the rest of our limited lives."

Thus, my boy's journey to the Central and South Americas was a done deal.

Then, my boy handed in his resignation. His boss had got wind of it all, and, alternately threatening and beseeching, tried to dissuade him from his decision. Finally, seeing that his decision was unchangeable, the boss even generously offered to give him a long vacation. But my boy said magnificently, "A man should follow his

水。何況，老闆不知民生疾苦，只要一聲令下，苦的可是我那些可憐的小主管、同事與下屬。」

聽起來像是古之義士。雖然不免覺得一份好端端的工作辭了可惜，卻也為他有擔當的作風感到驕傲。年終的股票沒了！每月孝敬我們的三分之一薪水飛了！我們咬牙佯裝豁達：

「錢再賺就有了！人生可只有一回。」

可不是人生只有一回嗎！病弱的外婆終究等不及孫子成行，在大年初三撒手仙逝。兒子履踐他幫外婆澆花的承諾，回潭子外婆家照顧院子的花花草草。在外婆說的「闊隆隆」的透天厝裡，一邊學習西班牙語，一邊準備各項資料，更重要的是陪伴並安撫離情依依的女友。外婆百日過後，他終於帶著一只大背包

principles and should not let his personal enjoyment outweigh the benefits of the whole company. Besides, the boss does not know how things are actually done. He only knows how to give orders, and the burden of carrying out his orders falls on those poor junior executives, my colleagues and their subordinates."

He sounded like some righteous man in the ancient world. Though I found it a pity for him to give up a good job, I was also proud of my boy's being a principled man. Gone were the annual stock dividends! Gone was the one-third of his monthly salary that went to me and his dad! We gritted our teeth and pretended all was well: "One can always make more money, but one only has one life."

"One only has one life," indeed! My boy's granny, weakened by her illness, did not live to see her grandchild embark on his grand tour. She passed away on the third day of the Chinese New Year. My boy moved in granny's house in Tanzi and fulfilled his promise to water those flowers for her. Staying in granny's sure-is-huge house, my boy started learning Spanish, prepared all the required documents, and, more importantly, accompanied and comforted

和幾張金融卡、信用卡瀟瀟上路。

　　臨走的那個黃昏，我們在福華麗香苑的沙拉吧給他餞行。該與不該叮嚀的話早都說完了，許是大夥兒都還沒從外婆往生的悲痛中恢復，場面顯得有些冷清、寂寥，也或許是我們夫妻倆的臉孔看起來有些僵硬，兒子打哈哈地安慰我們：

　　「去年，有一位身材瘦小的女性朋友，和我一樣揹著一口大背包出國雲遊，她媽媽到機場送行時，交代了又交代，拚命忍住眼眶裡含著的淚。過海關後，她一轉身，看見爸媽兩人的臉統統縮得小小的，眼睛顯得格外大且驚恐，她差點兒心軟地回頭。結果呢？上山下海一年浪遊後，還不是平平安安的回來。」

his girlfriend, who was beginning to feel the pain of separation from him. One hundred days after granny passed away, my boy, with a big backpack and several ATM cards and credit cards, went on his journey like a savvy traveler.

On the eve of his departure, my husband and I dined with him at Champs Elysees of the Howard Plaza Hotel and wished him Godspeed. We had said more than was necessary to remind him of what he should do when staying abroad. Then, perhaps not having recovered from the bereavement of granny's death, we began to feel a bit sad and lonely. My boy tried to comfort us and said, laughing, "Last year, a petite female friend of mine went on a journey with a big backpack, just like what I am about to do. Her mother saw her off at the airport, holding back tears and keeping reminding her of what she should do when staying abroad. Then, my friend went through Customs, turned around, and found that her parents' faces seemed very small and that their eyes dilated with fear. She almost changed her mind at that moment. And then what happened? After spending one year traveling around, she came back safe and sound."

一年後？外子和我同時驚詫地複述著，原本想要安慰我們的，卻因為這「一年後」三個字，引起我們更大的焦慮。但是，為了不顯示出太過保守或纏綿，身為爸媽的我們決定不在這個話題上窮追猛打。孩子大了，遠走高飛是遲早的事。只是，想到剛經歷了和母親的死別，隨即又得面對兒子的生離，臨別擁抱時，心情真是格外悽愴；兒子用手拍拍我的背，保證道：

「不用擔心，我會想辦法平安歸來的。」

母親走了，不知去了何方！兒子緊接著遠走他鄉！去到我沒辦法想像的南美洲，而我也糊裡糊塗接到新學校的聘書，即將變換跑道。一張張學生致贈的卡片，寫滿了捨不得我離開的字句，讓我閱之肝腸寸斷。幾個重大的變化接踵而至，攪得我手忙腳亂，心裡亂糟糟。幸而學期已近尾聲，學生忙於準備期末考，我倉皇搬離窩了九年的研究室，打包時，心情既

"After spending one year?" my husband and I repeated these words with astonishment. Instead of feeling comforted, we grew even more anxious, because of the words "after spending one year". But we decided to ignore these four little words, in order not to seem like overly conservative parents or those suffering from empty nest syndrome. I knew that sooner or later children had to start lives of their own. But I had just experienced the death of my mother, and now I had to face the departure of my boy. The day he left, I was extremely grieved when I gave my boy the parting hug. My boy patted my back and promised, "Don't worry. I will be home safe and sound."

My mother had gone to God knows where! Then my boy went to South America, a continent beyond my imagination! And now I was hired by a new university and was to begin a new chapter of my life. My students sent me many cards saying how they would like me to stay, and their tender words broke my heart. Major changes in life came one after another, and I was overwhelmed by them both physically and psychologically. Luckily, the semester was drawing to an end, and students were busy preparing for their final exams. Hurriedly, I moved out of my office where I had spent

繾綣又忐忑，像是無端被發配到不可測的遠方！當初只是想幫生病的母親打氣，成全她長久以來念茲在茲要我轉到公立大學的心願，如今，如願了，母親卻來不及知曉，留下我獨自面對茫茫的未來。

因為捨不得老家易主，我在母親往生之前，便將坐落潭子的老家買下，兒子走後的一個月，我將研究室囤積的書籍搬回潭子，發現花兒全凋謝了！葉子垂頭喪氣，水池內的魚兒暴斃了好幾條，院子裡的紅磚地灰撲撲的，曾經是母親病中魂牽夢縈、一心歸去的家，竟是一片荒蕪了。我杵在以前常跟母親坐著聊天、賞花的石椅前，內心慘怛，哽咽吞聲。夜裡，母親和兒子一起來入夢，翌日，我捎了封信給兒子，說：

……聽你女友說，她可能到玻利維亞找你；聽妹

the past nine years. As I packed my things, my heart was filled with longing for the past and anxiety for the future. I felt like an innocent person about to be deported to an unknown, distant country! Originally I just wanted to cheer up my mother, who was ill and had cherished a wish that I should teach at a national university. Now her wish was fulfilled, but she would never know about it. I alone was left to face my uncertain future.

Before my mother passed away, I bought the old house in Tanzi, because I could not bear to see it pass into the hands of some stranger. One month after my boy left Taiwan, I moved my books from my office to the house, and I found that the flowers had all withered and the leaves drooped. Many fish in the pond had died, and the red brick floor of the backyard was thick with dust. The home to which my mother in her illness had dreamt of returning was now in ruins. I stood in front of the stone chairs where my mother and I used to sit and talk and a look at her flowers. Grief-stricken, I cried in silence. At night, my mother and my boy came to me in my dream. The next day, I wrote a letter to my boy, saying, "... *I heard from your girlfriend that she probably would come to you in Bolivia; I heard from your sister that you were learning*

妹說，你正學西班牙文；聽我的夢境說，你爬了好幾座高山，因此扭傷了腰；在帆船上耍寶，差點兒掉進海裡……不知道這些都是真的嗎？

　　我昨天重新看了四年前到中研院訪問詩人楊牧的文章，他說起多年前曾提到的「壯遊」，他說：「我在《一首詩的完成》裡頭提到「壯遊」，其實我好像也不太贊成那樣子。我覺得跑來跑去幹什麼，一下子去巴西、一下子去布拉格，我覺得不見得有那個必要。不過讀書大概還是要，讀書是一種想像力的訓練。」

　　我引這段話的意思，不是打擊你的志氣，只是湊巧看到，想到這本書的出版，少說已有十多年，十多年前，詩人還大力鼓吹『壯遊』對寫詩的重要，十多年後，也許因為年紀的關係，他開始不大覺得此事有何重要。不過，趁年輕的時候有能力（包括體力和財

Spanish; in my dreams, you have climbed many high mountains and thus hurt your waist, or you are acting funny to amuse people on a sailboat and almost fall into the ocean… are these things real?

"Yesterday I read the article I wrote about interviewing the poet Yang Mu at the Academic Sinica. In that interview, he mentioned that he had talked about 'grand tours' many years ago. He said, 'I mention "grand tours" in The Completion of a Poem. *Come to think of it, maybe I don't actually approve of taking grand tours. I don't find it necessary to travel around the world, spending some time, for example, first in Brazil and then in Prague. But I guess people still need to read, for reading exercises their imagination.'*

"I did not mean to discourage you by quoting from Yang Mu. I just happened to read it. And it occurred to me that Yang's book had been published for at least more than a decade. More than a decade ago, Yang Mu preached the importance of taking 'grand tours' for poetry-writing. And more than a decade on, maybe because he was getting old, Yang began to think that grand tours were not that important after

力）到處走走看看，我和你爸爸倒是都很贊成的，只要你能保持清明的心智，注意防範意外，我們基本上是給予最大的支持的。

兒子對這番委婉的剴切言辭，視若無睹，全無回應。一個多月後，他的女友果然決定動身前去陪伴（或監督？），也辭了教書的工作，迢迢奔赴。有人同行，我們總算放心多了。兒子出門前，許多朋友聽說了，都警告我中南美是個落後、缺乏秩序的地方，要我轉告他得步步為營。兒子去了秘魯一段時間後，來信說一切都十分圓滿，秘魯根本不像大夥兒說的那樣危險、恐怖，要我們不用擔心！哪裡料到，這約莫就是所謂的「風雨前的寧靜」，其實危機已然四伏。一日，凌晨兩點鐘左右，朦朧正要進入夢鄉，忽然鈴聲大作，電話那頭傳來兒子氣急敗壞的聲音，說是只在市集中點了幾道吃食，一回頭，背包已經被偷，所

all. However, your dad and I quite approve of your decision to travel around the world while you are young and can afford it (in terms of your physical and financial conditions). As long as you stay sensible and take precautions against accidents, basically we will give you our fullest support."

My boy did not find my euphemistic admonition worthy of a reply. More than a month later, his girlfriend did resign from her teaching position and traveled a long way to accompany (or maybe supervise) him. We felt much relieved now that someone kept him company there. Before my boy's departure, many friends had heard about his decision, warned me how under-developed, chaotic the Central and South Americas were, and wanted me to advise my boy to be careful of every step he takes there. Having spent some time in Peru, my boy sent me a letter, saying how everything went well and how Peru was not as terrible and dangerous as he had been told and we should not worry about him. Little did we know that it was merely "peace before the storm." And the storm came. One day, when I was about to fall asleep, I heard the phone ringing incessantly. My boy phoned and said tempestuously that, having ordered something to eat in the market, he turned around

以，請我們連夜為他的提款卡、簽帳卡辦理止付。被這一攪和，我睡意全消，辦過手續後，竟睜眼到天明。第二天，接到兒子的E-Mail，列出損失清單，總計：

「iPod一台、美國簽證一份、貴重夾克一件、照相機一部、記憶卡三張、尚未儲存的照片4GB、LV皮夾一只、信用卡、金融卡各兩張、notebook（中有珍貴日記）一台、新買背包一個及帽子一頂……其他族繁不及備載。」

他在信裡幾度重申：
「真是恨得牙癢癢的……」

看完之後，不禁莞爾，想到彈藥已被鎖進彈藥庫，也許他會因彈盡援絕而提早歸來。正當我將這不足為外人道的竊喜告訴兒子時，他哈哈大笑，說：
「正好相反！因為許多的紀錄與照片都毀於一

and found his backpack stolen. He asked us to contact the banks to suspend his ATM cards and credit cards. After I went through all the procedures, no trace of sleepiness was to be found, and I did not sleep all night. The next day, my boy sent me email, listing what had been stolen, "an iPod, my visa to America, a very expensive jacket, a camera, three memory cards with four giga bytes of photos, an LV wallet, two credit cards, two ATM cards, a notebook with my precious diary in it, a new backpack, a hat, etc. "

Over and over he says in the mail, "Dang the thief…"

Having read the mail, I could not help smiling. Now my boy was like a soldier out of ammunition with no relief forces in sight, and maybe he would decide to come home earlier than he had planned. When I shared my private joy with my boy, he laughed boisterously and said, "Quite on the contrary! Because I have lost

旦，所以，可能延長歸期以補回那些遺失的日子⋯⋯
可不可以麻煩你們先墊些錢寄到女友的帳戶裡？」

　　真是太讓人失望了！既知孺子頑固不可教，我遂
將眼光轉向潭子的老家。母親雖然走了，相信她可不
希望庭園敗壞，家人四散、兄妹各行其是。於是，趁
著暑假，我和外子展開另類的耕種生活。每天像苦行
僧般，披頭散髮種花、種樹、種竹子；洗衣、洗被、
洗院子；拖地、擦窗、曬被子；釘鉤、掛畫、掛簾
子；搬土、搬磚、搬盆子！每天汗流浹背，汗水像雨
水般灑下，不要命似的工作，腰也彎了，人也黑了。
我們將大門進來左方的大片水泥地敲開，種了三株四
方竹，芭樂樹、芒果樹、檸檬、奇異果各一棵，幾株
聖女番茄，還在小池裡養了幾盆蓮花、池邊植了柳
樹，大缸裡種了荷花，棚架旁兩株巨峰葡萄迎風招
展，外子還修了摩托車、買了腳踏車，屋裡安上新窗

many records and photos, I may have to stay longer to make up for the stolen time. … Could you lend me some money and deposit it into my girlfriend's account?"

I was sorely disappointed. Since my boy was such an intractable "prodigal son," I turned my attention to the old house in Tanzi. It's true that my mother had gone, but she would not want to see the house in ruins, the family scattered, and siblings concerned only about their own business. So, during the summer vacation, my husband and I began some sort of agricultural life. Like some ascetic monks, and with our hairs unkempt, we planted flowers, trees, and bamboos. We washed our clothes and bed quilts, and we cleaned the backyard. We mopped the floors, wiped the windows, and hung out the quilts. We clinched nails and hung some paintings and curtains. We removed dirt, bricks and pots. Everyday our sweat poured like rain. We worked unsparingly, our backs bent and our skins tanned. We cracked the large concrete floor that could be seen on your left-hand side when you entered the gate, and we planted there three square bamboos, one guava tree, one mango tree, one lemon tree, one kiwi tree, and some mini tomatoes. We also kept some potted water lilies in a pond and

簾、方桌鋪上桌巾、裝上音響；那樣子，像是要在潭子老家長住久居。我讓女兒拍了各個角度的美美照片寄去玻利維亞，引誘兒子：

院子經過一番整理，煥然一新；客廳的日曆及月曆被取下，換上雷驤伯伯的裸女畫、華仁叔叔的鳥類版畫和爸爸的小幅風景畫作，人文氣息立刻浮現。等你們回來時，也許不但可以摘葡萄、釀葡萄酒，還可以爬芭樂樹，嘴裡吃著芒果、番茄，眼裡看著依依的楊柳、田田的荷葉和精神煥發的蘭花，坐在竹林下成為七賢之一……爸爸已把大畫布搬回潭子，打算在葡萄架下畫出驚世之作，我們正拭目以待。

planted some willows next to it. Some lotuses were kept in a large pot, and the two kyoho grapes on lattice danced in the wind. My husband fixed his motorcycle and bought a bicycle. New curtains were hung in the house, table clothes were laid, and a stereo set was installed. It all looked as if we planned to live in the old house in Tanzi for a long time. I asked my daughter to take pictures of the house from different angles and send these beautiful pictures to Bolivia to entice my boy back:

"The backyard has been rearranged and looks refreshed. The daily and monthly calendars have been replaced by uncle Lei Hsiang's paintings of nude women, uncle He Huaren's avian engravings and dad's small landscape paintings, endowing the living room with humanistic elegance. When you are back, maybe you can pick some grapes, brew some wine, or climb the guava tree. You can also enjoy some mangoes and tomatoes, while looking at the delicate willows, the verdant lotus leaves, and the sprightly orchids. Sitting in the bamboo forest, you can imagine yourself to be one of the seven intellectuals in the Jin dynasty. ... Dad has moved that large canvas of his to Tanzi, and he intends to sit under the grape vines and paint on the canvas something really extraordinary. We all look forward to his painting."

　　兒子雖表達驚豔之意，卻仍然鎮靜以對，依然叨叨敘說著世界之大、他鄉山河的美好壯麗、異地人情的種種。我有些失落，心裡的某處像是被鑿了個大窟窿，空空洞洞的，在屋裡踱過來走過去，老覺心神不寧。

　　中秋長假之始，我召回散居各處的兄姊及其家人，大大小小，合計接近二十口人，炒米粉、買來鵝肉、端出媽媽最拿手的紅燒肉、筍乾，摘下院子裡的九層塔炒茄子，也沒忘記我最專長的什錦菜，我跟母親生前一樣，待在廚房裡，細細切絲、大火熱炒，把廚房搞得熱騰騰、火辣辣……前廳有人打麻將，有人聊天，中小孩看電視、打電腦；小小孩拿著手電筒四處奔來跑去，還有人在院子裡烤香腸，依然熱熱鬧鬧的一家人，彷彿母親從來沒有離開過。夜深了，人散了，我像母親一樣，打開櫃子，拿出幾罐茶葉；從冰

My boy said he was pleasantly surprised by what had happened to the old house, but he remained perfectly calm, talking over and over about the big world, the spectacular scenery of exotic countries, and the habits and customs of foreign people. I felt somewhat lost. It was as if some part of my heart had been removed, and a big, empty hole was left there. Pacing to and fro in the old house, I often felt perturbed, restless.

At the beginning of the long Moon Festival Vacation, I gathered together my siblings and their families, there being nearly twenty of them of different generations. I bought some cooked duck meat, and I prepared stir-fried rice noodles and my mom's specialty dishes, braised pork and dried bamboo shoots. I also prepared stir-fried eggplants with Chinese basil leaves gathered from the backyard. And I did not forget to prepare my own special assorted dish. Like my mom, I stayed in the kitchen, and sliced and stir-fried the ingredients. As a result, the kitchen was heated and hot. ... In the front room, some people played mah-jongg, and some other people chatted. The teens watched TV and played computer games; the even younger kids ran around with flashlights in their hands. And still some other people roasted sausages in the backyard. In the

箱上層取出儲備的魚、肉；下層翻出青菜、蔬果和剩菜，分別打包，讓各家帶回。汽車一部一部駛離，我像昔日的母親一樣，將頭伸進開著的車窗，交代駕駛人：「小心開車哦！免趕緊！」然後，站在紅門口揮手道別，車子緩緩陸續開出巷口，我抬頭看到天空上寥落的星星一閃一閃的，淚水忽然像泉湧，母親的心情，從來沒有一刻像當下那般分明！

雖然疲累不堪，心情卻是亢奮的。我慫恿女兒將紅燒肉、炒米粉、筍乾等食物的照片，用MSN遞送到天涯海角，並隨圖附上幾句話：

每逢佳節倍思親，我思我父我母，更思人在遠方的我子，而你莫非樂不思蜀？可別忘了蜀地的父老日

cheerful hustle and bustle, everyone acted as one family, as if mom had never left. The night progressed, and the family gathering drew to an end. Like my mom, I opened the cabinet and took out from it several jars of tea leaves; I took out some reserved fish and meat from the upper room of the refrigerator; I took out vegetables, fruit and leftovers from the lower room of the refrigerator. I packed and distributed all these things. As the cars began to drive away one by one, I, like my mom, stuck my head into the cars and enjoined the drivers, "Be careful when you drive! There is no need to rush!" Then, standing next to the red gate, I waved goodbye to them. The cars slowly disappeared one by one from the corner of the lane. I looked up, saw some scattered stars twinkling, and suddenly my tears gushed. Never had I felt so distinctly what being a mother was like.

I was physically exhausted but emotionally excited. I urged my daughter to send pictures of braised pork, stir-fried rice noodles and dried bamboo shoots to the other end of the world through MSN. Accompanying the pictures were the following words:

"We miss those dear to us all the more on festival days. I miss my father, I miss my mother, and I miss even more my boy in the distance. But have you been enjoying too much fun to even remember those

日引頸盼望，就怕兒子浪蕩成習，成了天涯流浪漢。今天的月亮很圓，想你猶然羈旅海外，家人都讓院子裡的炭火嗆出了淚來了。

兒子想是被油亮的紅燒肉給感動了，立即引用了孟老夫子的話來回應中文系出身的老母，說：

天將降大任於斯人也，必先苦其心志，勞其筋骨，餓其體膚，空乏其身，行拂亂其所為。」漢客在南美過的是困苦的日子，每天用半冷不熱的水洗浴，在此無一刻不思念家鄉的麻辣鍋、牛肉麵與肉圓，您傳來的爌肉配米粉更是讓人垂涎，但在南半球的月亮盈虧與北半球不同，能夠換個角度看世界，換取人生經驗，這樣的困苦又算些什麼！十分想念老父老母，一切可好？

流浪漢Hank

waiting for you at home? Don't forget those at home who pray that their boy do not turn into a wandering prodigal son. The moon is round tonight. And you are in a foreign country and not with us. Thinking of this separation, your family members have been choked into tears by the fumes from the burning coals."

Maybe my boy was touched by that braised pork. Immediately he replied to his mother, educated in the Department of Chinese Literature, with a quote from Mencius.

"Mencius said, 'Before one can assume great responsibility from the Divine Sovereignty, one must first have one' mind tormented, one's limbs exhausted, one's body famished, one's possessions depleted, and one's endeavors thwarted.' I have lived in poverty in South America, bathing in lukewarm water everyday. Not a day goes by without me missing those hometown delicacies, like spicy hot pot, beef noodles, meat dumplings, and especially stir-fried rice noodles with braised pork (I saw it in one of the pictures you sent me). But the moon in the southern hemisphere waxes and wanes differently from what it does in the northern hemisphere. What do all these problems matter, if I get to see the world from a different perspective and gain more experiences in life? I miss you and dad very much. Hope all is well with you.

　　四兩撥千斤的，兒子輕易就掙脫了我撒下的密密親情網罟，身手矯健地脫身而出，若無其事地繼續他在遠方的天涯追尋。

　　中秋那天清晨，女兒起了個大早，忽然在院子拉開嗓門呼叫：

　　「媽！您趕快來看！很奇怪呢，九月天竟然開出一朵粉紅的杜鵑花。」

　　我穿著睡衣、睜著惺忪的睡眼跑出去，看到久不開花的院落，獨獨開出了一朵小小的粉紅杜鵑花，怎麼都沒注意到何時結的花苞！我不知道一向開在「淡淡的三月天」的杜鵑花，是否經過改良而能在任何的季節綻放，但是，花開一朵，靜靜地藏身枝葉間，卻讓我感覺它彷彿是個特別的神蹟。分明是琵琶半遮面

Your wandering child,
Hank

I had hoped to capture my boy with a well-wrought net of familial intimacy, but effortlessly and nimbly he escaped and continued his quest in the distance as if nothing had happened.

On the morning of the Moon Festival, my daughter woke up early, and suddenly she shouted in the backyard, "Mom! Quick! Come to see this! How strange it is that a pink azalea blossoms in September. "

Still wearing my pajamas, I ran out of my room with sleepy eyes and saw, in the backyard that had for so long not been blessed with blossoms, a tiny pink azalea. I had not even noticed when the flower was in bud! I had no idea whether or not azaleas had been genetically modified so that they could blossom not just in the mild March weather but in all seasons. But, seeing just one flower hiding in silence among the leaves, I seemed to witness a special miracle.

的「欲言又止」模樣！難道一向愛花、愛熱鬧的母親果真成了花神？藉由單開一枝的花朵來嘉許我促成全家再度團聚的苦心嗎？

　　那夜，母親迢迢來入夢。夢中的母親依然孱弱，枯瘦的身子和我併肩站在大片落地窗前，窗外細雨霏霏，遠處一脈橫臥的蔥綠高山，近處是挨擠著的長排豔紅美人蕉，像極一張濕淋淋的素雅彩畫。母親不堪久站，將頭倚在我的肩頭，神情愉悅且滿足地說：「真正是極美啊！」然後，頭一歪，似是沉沉睡去一般。我也不驚惶，好像理當如此，就這樣讓母親靠著，兩人一直靠著、靠著……

　　「母親累了，睡了，就讓她靠著多睡一會兒吧！」

And it seemed that the flower wished to say something to me and yet hesitated. Was it that my mother, who had loved flowers and enjoyed the hustle and bustle of life, was now a goddess of flowers and wished, with that one flower, to compliment me on my efforts to bring the family together?

That night, my mother traveled a long way to visit me in my dream. She was still weak and skinny and stood shoulder to shoulder with me in front of a large French window. Tiny rain drops pounded intensively on the window. In the distance could be seen a verdant mountain ridge and, somewhere near us, a long, crowded row of canna lilies in eye-opening red. All looked like a drenched watercolor painting. My mother could not stand up for too long, so she leaned her head on my shoulder. Joyfully and contentedly she said, "It all looks so very beautiful!" Then her head moved slightly askew, and she seemed to fall into a sound sleep. I had no fears, as if things were as they should be. I let my mother lean on me, and I leaned on her…

"Mom is tired. Let her sleep. Let her lean on my shoulder and sleep for a while. "

我在夢裡如此寬慰自己。

中夜醒來，肩頭隱隱痠麻，我愣坐著，覺得母親真的回來過了，回想她觀花時的滿足表情，彷彿告訴我：遠方並不可怕。

──原載二〇〇七年十月十九、二十日《聯合報》

收入九歌版《後來》（2011年）

I comforted myself in my dream.

I woke up in the middle of the night, my shoulder slightly numb. I sat there doing nothing. And it felt like my mom had really paid me a visit. I tried to remember her contented expression when looking at the flowers. That expression seemed to tell me, "There is nothing to fear in the distance."

讀名家・學英文02

繁華散盡：
廖玉蕙散文中英對照

作者	廖玉蕙
譯者	胡守芳、湯麗明、謝孟宗等
責任編輯	宋敏菁
發行人	蔡文甫
出版發行	九歌出版社有限公司
	臺北市105八德路3段12巷57弄40號
	電話／02-25776564・傳真／02-25789205
	郵政劃撥／0112295-1
九歌文學網	www.chiuko.com.tw
印刷	晨捷印製股份有限公司
法律顧問	龍躍天律師・蕭雄淋律師・董安丹律師
初版	2011（民國100）年4月
定價	**300元**

書號	V0002
ISBN	978-957-444-760-2

（缺頁、破損或裝訂錯誤，請寄回本公司更換）

國家圖書館出版品預行編目資料

繁華散盡：廖玉蕙散文中英對照／廖玉蕙著；
胡守芳等譯. -- 初版. -- 台北市：九歌，
民100.04
　　面；　　公分
ISBN　978-957-444-760-2（平裝）

855　　　　　　　　　　　　　　100003140